Bent on Revenge

It took damn near all of Longarm's rapidly dwindling strength to get a grip on the screeching female, then pull her off his wild-eyed, thrashing prisoner. He dragged the red-faced Billie to the jail's front entry and pushed her toward the boardwalk.

To Longarm's shocked dismay, the thrashing female stumbled over the doorway's raised threshold, floundered, then fell in a crumpled heap and rolled into Val Verde's fancy stone-paved street. A group of townsfolk witnessed the whole unfortunate affair.

When Longarm swung his attention to the grumbling crowd, a lanky tough, wearing a Texas-style Stetson and a profoundly indignant look, had grabbed the scrambling Billie by one arm and was working to steady her efforts to stand.

She glowered at Longarm and snapped, "That ugly bastard in there murdered my little brother, mister. And I intend to see he pays for his crime. Get in the way and you just might not live much longer yourself."

DON'T MISS THESE
ALL-ACTION WESTERN SERIES
FROM THE BERKLEY PUBLISHING GROUP

TABOR EVANS

LONGARM AND THE VAL VERDE MASSACRE

J

JOVE BOOKS, NEW YORK

THE BERKLEY PUBLISHING GROUP
Published by the Penguin Group
Penguin Group (USA) Inc.
375 Hudson Street, New York, New York 10014, USA
Penguin Group (Canada), 90 Eglinton Avenue East, Suite 700, Toronto, Ontario M4P 2Y3, Canada
(a division of Pearson Penguin Canada Inc.)
Penguin Books Ltd., 80 Strand, London WC2R 0RL, England
Penguin Group Ireland, 25 St. Stephen's Green, Dublin 2, Ireland (a division of Penguin Books Ltd.)
Penguin Group (Australia), 250 Camberwell Road, Camberwell, Victoria 3124, Australia
(a division of Pearson Australia Group Pty. Ltd.)
Penguin Books India Pvt. Ltd., 11 Community Centre, Panchsheel Park, New Delhi—110 017, India
Penguin Group (NZ), 67 Apollo Drive, Rosedale, North Shore 0632, New Zealand
(a division of Pearson New Zealand Ltd.)
Penguin Books (South Africa) (Pty.) Ltd., 24 Sturdee Avenue, Rosebank, Johannesburg 2196, South Africa

Penguin Books Ltd., Registered Offices: 80 Strand, London WC2R 0RL, England

LONGARM AND THE VAL VERDE MASSACRE

A Jove Book / published by arrangement with the author

PRINTING HISTORY
Jove edition / June 2009

Cover illustration by Miro Sinovcic.

For information, address: The Berkley Publishing Group,
a division of Penguin Group (USA) Inc.,
375 Hudson Street, New York, New York 10014.

ISBN: 978-0-515-14640-0

JOVE®
Jove Books are published by The Berkley Publishing Group,
a division of Penguin Group (USA) Inc.,
375 Hudson Street, New York, New York 10014.
JOVE® is a registered trademark of Penguin Group (USA) Inc.
The "J" design is a trademark of Penguin Group (USA) Inc.

PRINTED IN THE UNITED STATES OF AMERICA

10 9 8 7 6 5 4 3 2 1

Chapter 1

Billy Vail's often testy secretary didn't even bother to look up from his fancy new typewriting contrivance when his boss's favorite deputy, Custis Long, strode into the U.S. marshal's outer office and reception area. The red-faced, overworked, put-upon administrator simply threw an off-hand wave in Longarm's direction and said, "Go right in, Deputy Long. Our beset, bothered, and bewildered leader has an abundance of blazing-hot irons in the fire this morning. He should be with you shortly, though."

Longarm snatched off his snuff-colored, flat-crowned Stetson, started for Vail's inner sanctum, then stopped in the doorway. A sly grin played across his ruggedly handsome face. The prospect of playfully ruffling the feathers of Vail's underling proved too good a morning's entertainment to pass up.

"Where the hell is he? Thought this was some kind of emergency. Urgent note I got said to drop everything and get myself on over here quick as I could. Hell, Henry, I *dropped* something real important to get here this fast. Real important. 'Pears it's just another case of hurry up and wait."

The tickety-tackety fall of the typing machine's print heads against paper and feed roll abruptly stopped. A fleeting, cantankerous grimace flickered across the preoccupied secretary's thin lips. Then, he resumed hunting and pecking at the inlaid-ivory pads of his noisy contraption. "What was her name?" he called out over the clicking and clacking.

"Whose name?" Longarm said, as though innocent as the proverbial newborn babe.

"The *name* of the *something important* you dropped in order to get from your palatial digs down on Cherry Creek all the way up here to Denver's Federal District Court building so quick. *That* name, Deputy Marshal Long." After a second's pause, under his breath, Henry added, "Hope you didn't hurt her when you dropped the lady."

Longarm stared at the toes of his low-heeled, freshly buffed and polished cordovan leather boots. Then he cast a bemused gaze up at the reception area's fancy, embossed tin ceiling. He scratched his chin, as though lost in deep, concentrated thought. "Well, now, my attention ain't always focused on a woman, you know. I do have other important concerns that often weigh heavily on my mind, Henry. Yes indeed, important concerns."

"Truly?"

"Oh, absolutely. Might not realize it, but you're in the presence of a man burdened, heavily burdened as a matter of pure fact, by an abundance of significant and arduous affairs. Kinds of dealings that require my undivided attention during those infrequent times I'm able to have a few days away from chasin' badmen and badwomen in bad places. And gettin' shot at, sometimes beaten senseless, thrown from horses. Occasionally bit by snakes, or hideous poisonous insect-type critters, in the prosecution of my mandate, I might, by God, add."

"Significant affairs? That's a good one—more like crawling your way around Denver, frequenting even more questionable establishments than the run-of-the-mill saloons, drinking yourself into a stupor, gambling, and womanizing, I'd wager. But that's beside the point. In typical Longarm fashion, you're dodging my original question," Henry said, then snapped a sheet of ivory-toned, linen paper from the rubber-rollered loading apparatus on his new-fangled writing device. He stared at the dense, word-crowded sheet for several seconds, then dropped it into a wooden tray on the far corner of his desk.

"Not true, my dear Henry. It's just that, even if an overly friendly lady happened to have been the *primary occupation* of my morning, it would not be chivalrous for a gentleman of my strict cavalier upbringing to discuss her with a lowly, pencil-pushing, typewriting federal office worker such as yourself." Having thrown down the verbal gauntlet, so to speak, Longarm grinned into his hat, then knifed another squinty-eyed glance in the overly sensitive Henry's direction and waited.

"*Lowly, pencil-pushing, typewriting federal office worker*, huh? I'm going to remember that snide comment the next time you're stuck out on the ragged edge of Less Than Nowhere, Arizona, or Ass Whistle, Texas, and burning up the telegraph wires seeking my assistance."

Longram toed at the thick rug beneath his feet like a contrite child. "Well, now, you might be right. Please let me offer up my sincerest apologies for that untoward remark, Henry. Just kinda slipped out, as it were. Loose mouth got ahead of a sleep-besotted brain. Hope you'll forgive my rude, unthinking remarks."

Before Vail's assistant could formulate another pithy, stinging response in their verbal dueling match, the U.S. marshal stormed in. He stomped past Longarm with his nose buried in a thick sheaf of fluttering documents. Didn't bother to look up when he flew past and said, "Come on into the office, Custis. Take your regular seat. Need to get you movin' quick as we can."

Hat in hand, Longarm pointed a gunlike finger at the grinning Henry and feigned pulling the trigger. Then he hurriedly followed his preoccupied boss through the open doorway to the proffered seat in front of Vail's massive, overburdened desk.

Longarm flopped into the well-used, tack-decorated, Moroccan leather guest's chair. Crossed one leg over the other. Then flipped his recently cleaned and reblocked Stetson onto the toe of a boot so luminously buffed he could see his own face in the sheen. Surly scamp who'd polished his footwear had done a damned fine job. For about a second, Longarm wondered if he had tipped the rascal enough. He thumped a speck of dust off one heel, then refocused his attention onto his agitated supervisor.

Vail sagged into the banker's chair behind his desk. He shoved a mountain of other documents aside, then continued to peruse the contents of his newest bundle of papers. Engrossed man didn't look up for several seconds. Finally, he pitched the stack aside, pinched the bridge of his nose, and groaned. He muttered something unintelligible, then contemplated his fingernails as though he might whip out a penknife and take time to give them a good cleaning.

After several seconds of silence, the tired-looking U.S. marshal glanced at his deputy, scrunched down in his seat, and said, "Sorry you had to wait, Custis. Got a committee of meddlesome U.S. senators poking around the building. Typical of the breed, they're asking the damned stupidest questions a reasonable body could ever think up, and being a general set of unneeded pains in my tired, aching ass. There's not a damned one of the whole group that wouldn't have to study for two or three years to be a half-wit. Hell, even a quarter-wit."

Longarm twisted in his seat. "Oh, God. Do feel for you, Billy. Can't quite reach you, but I do feel for you. So, guess we might as well get this over with so I can get the hell outta here. Wouldn't want to encounter any of them quarter-wits myself unless absolutely necessary. Not sure I could ever exercise your kind of talent with diplomatic tact."

Vail angrily ran the fingers of one hand back and forth through his thinning hair, as if he might dig through his own skull and pluck out a chunk of brain. "Honest to God,

Custis, think the Congress of these United States has an active investigative committee for every pissant problem imaginable. Wouldn't surprise me to find out there's an agency of the Senate or the House that studies nothing but construction specifications for two-hole shitters located on federal property and equipped with some kind of newfangled, electric-powered, automatic ass-wiping device."

Longarm snorted into his fist and tried not to laugh out loud.

"Actually, I'm kinda glad we had to call this conference," Vail said. "Gave me a good reason to tell that pack of nabobs that I had a very important meeting and it could not be delayed. Was more than happy to excuse myself from their collectively idiotic company for a few minutes."

"Senators, huh? Seems like there's a bunch a them nitpickin' sons a bitches pokin' into somethin' or other every time we turn around, Billy."

"Yeah, well, that's government for you. With every passing hour, seems like we get way more of it than anyone really needs. The *people* elect 'em. Then the sons a bitches get to Washington and feel like they've just got to do *something*. Folks out here in the field, like you and me, are forced to put up with 'em."

A thoughtful silence fell over the pair of old friends like a damp blanket in a snowstorm.

"Tell me, Custis," Vail said, as though tired to the bone, "do you think we'll ever get a handle on all the criminal activity and downright evil that takes place in areas of this country under our official purview?"

The question required not a single second of wasted thought on Longarm's part. "Oh, hell, no, Billy. There's about as much chance of that as August snowball fights in Nuevo Laredo. Ain't the slightest doubt about it, we're fixed for a life's worth of work here. Got so many stink-sprayin' skunks runnin' loose on the good folk of this part of the world, figure as how you'll probably be a-callin' me in to chase badmen down when I'm gettin' on up around ninety. Probably have to get your man Henry to push me through that door yonder in one a them chairs what has wheels on it for old geezers."

Vail slapped the top of his desk, hopped up, and strode to the window behind his chair. He pushed the heavy curtain aside with one finger and stared down onto the hustle and bustle of Colfax Avenue. A ray of muted sunlight sliced into the room, then quickly faded when he let the drapery panel slip back into place.

Like a field commander in the headquarters tent of an active army command, Vail did a smartly executed about-face, then said, "Swear 'fore Jesus, Custis, sometimes the world appears on a bobsled ride straight to fiery Perdition. And near as I can tell, not a single son of a bitch's working the brakes."

Longarm picked at a fingernail. "Other day I read an article in the Denver newspaper that recounted a buncha brutal murders committed by members of an entire family over in the Indian Nations."

"Musta missed that one. Say the whole clan was involved?"

"Yep. Seems as how this feller was using his wife and daughters as bait. Three young'uns was right good-lookin' gals as I recall. They was lurin' travelers into a night's stopover in the family's rustic home. Promise of lewd behavior and such if the passersby rented a room, I'd be willin' to bet."

"I've known of similar ruses in the past," Vail said, then slid back into his chair.

"Anyhow, under cover of darkness, the father'd sneak into the rooms of them poor ignorant goobers as couldn't control their own lechery. Kill 'em, rob 'em of all their valuables. Then he and the wife'd bury the body under a chicken coop out behind his house. Guess things were going along just swimmingly for the family business till a tougher'n-toenails feller from down 'round Uvalde decided as how he didn't care to die quite so young."

"Damn."

"Yeah, that ole South Texas boy fought like a cornered badger. Give the father, and the son, too, one helluva ass-whippin'. Got one a his paws lopped off with a choppin' ax for all his efforts to stay alive. Still managed to kill the son one-handed. Got the kid right betwixt the eyes with a .44."

"Have mercy."

"Most recently, local authorities indicated as how they've retrieved the smelly, decayin' remains of eight corpses. Some identified, some not. Most with holes in the skull from what is believed to have been a pickax. Lookin' for more of them poor dead folks, too. Maybe a lot more, bein' as how the murderin' bastard had several of them chicken houses on his property. 'S enough to put a man off his feed, you ask me. Just god-awful doin's goin' on out there, you know. Tell you, Billy, a sane person couldn't think of such."

"Help me, Jesus," Vail muttered.

"Yeah. Terrible doin's. Biblical, you ask me. But that ain't nothin' really."

"Not sure I want to hear any more."

"You started it. So, listen to this. Heard tell of a feller down on the Rio Grande what was pulling a similar ruse to that 'un in the Nations. But, hell, Billy, he was eatin' them as he murdered. Can you imagine? Piece I read, in the *Del Rio Sentinel*, recounted as how he'd butchered people like slaughterhouse cattle. Boiled 'em in a black iron kettle that he used durin' hog-killin' time out back of his place. Then he ate 'em. Claimed a bit of human hock was just by-God tastier'n all get out."

Vail rolled his eyes toward Heaven, as though seeking some kind of divine guidance, or at least a bit of relief from such unbridled madness. He leaned forward on both elbows and shook his head in disbelief.

"Suppose for some of the twisted, lunatic bastards out there lookin' to do mischief," Longarm said, "a nice piece of human haunch is just the thing when they sit down for an evening's meal. Ear of corn. Couple a taters. Some redeye gravy. Bit a human hip and thigh. Good goobly-oobly, Billy. Gives me the creepin' willies just tryin' to picture such a meal in my mind's eye."

Vail groaned, then tiredly ran one hand from forehead to chin. "Yeah, well, I've got another case for you, and you're gonna have to get going quick as you can. Henry should be about finished on the warrants, travel documents, advances, stipends, and such as we speak. Unfortunately, you don't have much time. Gonna have to get a move on. He's checked and tells me there's a train leaving for Fort Stockton in a matter of hours."

Longarm let out a groan like a wounded bear. "Aw, shit, Billy. Fort Stockton? Not kiddin', are you? Jesus, you know how I hate that place."

"Can't be helped."

"God Almighty. Ain't nothin' out there but tarantulas, rattlesnakes, scorpions, and Messicans. This time a year, it's hot 'nuff in West Texas to melt leather that's still attached to the steer. Hotter'n a jug full a red ants."

Vail flashed a strained grin and shook his head.

"Yeah, swear it's the truth," said Longarm. "Heard tell of a feller down in Eagle Pass that's feedin' his chickens cracked ice. Tryin' to see if he can keep 'em from layin' hard-boiled eggs."

Behind an ever-widening smile, Vail swatted Longarm's complaints and feeble attempts at humor aside with a single, chopping wave of the hand. "Just have to figure this Texas trip's nothing more than penance for that vacation you took up to Wyoming Territory month or so ago. That escapade's still costing me plenty in the way of expended time and energy."

A pained expression of feigned shock and dismay

flashed onto Longarm's animated visage. "Vacation? Penance? Sweet Virginia, Billy. Your already feeble memory must be slippin' on you. Gettin' a touch of the hardenin' of the arteries or somethin'. Too much time behind that desk. You ain't moving 'round enough, ole hoss. Hate to remind you, but I damn near bit the big one on that Wyoming trip. Jim Ed Cobb come nigh on to cuttin' me up like a Sunday chicken. Good God, Billy, they was a time or two durin' that little dustup got to figuring as how I just might end up with no more pulse than a pitchfork. Came close on to bein' deader'n Hell in a Baptist preacher's front vestibule."

Chapter 2

Billy Vail didn't have to be a Leadville mining engineer to figure out that the conversation between him and his favorite deputy had suddenly taken a definite change in direction.

Vail slid deeper into his overstuffed seat. Steepled his fingers, as though in deep thought for several seconds, then pulled a brass-embellished polished-wood humidor from the lowest drawer of the desk. Flipped the engraved lid open. Stretched across the mountains of paper between the pair. Offered Longarm one of his private stash of premium, gold-labeled El Presidente cigars.

Each and every one of those perfectly wrapped cylinders of aromatic, slightly greenish-tinted tobacco were as big around as a grown man's thumb. The manly smokes were painstakingly rolled on the dewy thighs of beautiful, hot-natured Cuban señoritas—at least that's what Vail liked to boast to any of those lucky enough to be offered one of those cigars. Given Custis Long's penchant for rum-dipped, dirt-cheap cheroots, this was quite a treat.

Vail placed the fancy box between them, wallowed out a comfortable spot in his seat again, then lit up. As a cloud of fragrant blue smoke floated over his head, he said, "Well, look Custis, if you mean the *little dustup*, as you've so cunningly called it, that occurred when you finally ran Cobb to ground in Le Beau, I'm still dealing with half a dozen or so citizen complaints about the mess you left in your wake. Can't really blame those folks myself. Most people just don't generally take to unexpected, nigh on total destruction."

Longarm leaned forward. He picked, shuffled, sniffed at, and finally selected a stogie from Vail's container of goodies. He ran the rich-smelling cigar back and forth beneath his nose. Thought of beautiful Cuban señoritas, licked the peppery-tasting wrapper, then stoked the cigar to life. A rising umbrella of full-bodied, steel-colored smoke enveloped his head. He picked a sprig of tobacco off his lip, then said, "Le Beau. Now, there's a real hoot. Funnier'n hell name for that particular town, I'll tell you for damned sure. 'S French, ain't it, Billy? Think the word translates out to somethin' like The Beautiful, or The Beauty. Gotta admit, my French ain't that great."

Vail added another wave to the roiling, fragrant ocean of grayish blue mist collecting near his office's ceiling. "Well, jeez, Wyoming Territory is by all accounts about as close as you can get to heaven on earth, Custis," he said, then flipped his dead match into a pewter ashtray atop the mound of litter between them. "Leastways, every part of it I've ever visited. But somehow, you strolled into Le Beau and managed to cause monumental problems in heaven."

"Le Beau's heaven on earth, huh? Well, that's bullshit. You obviously ain't never been up on the Rattlesnake River. Ankle-deep branch of the Chugwater. Ass-end of nowhere."

"That's a bit harsh. Don't you think?"

"Nope. And somethin' else. *Visited?* That's real damn funny, Billy. Trust me on this one. Le Beau ain't exactly the kinda place anyone would ever want to *visit.* Not the average Eastern tourist's preferred destination for rest, recuperation, or leisurely endeavors. One-dog burg's not even on any map as I've ever seen. If a body weren't lookin' hard for the place, couldn't find it with a jeweler's loop and a willow divining rod."

"Jeweler's loop. Now, I like that. Original."

"Ain't foolin' now. No, sir. Hellhole of the first order. Still have trouble tryin' to figure out why anyone in their right mind ever bothered to build a half-assed town up there in the middle of deserted nothingness in the first place."

"So, anyhow, you chased Jim Ed Cobb to the town of Le Beau on the Rattlesnake River in Wyoming Territory. And once you'd arrived, managed to piss off near'bouts half the settlement's citizenry before you finally took him into custody. Near as I've been able to determine, that bit of failed diplomacy only occupied about twenty minutes of your time all told."

Longarm sucked down a lungful of the fragrant, heavy cigar smoke, then blew a washtub-sized ring into the churning haze building against Billy Vail's ceiling like phantom waters lapping against a ghostly dam. "Well, I never *meant* to inflame the twenty or thirty good citizens of that peckerwood-sized hamlet. Never did. Swear 'fore Jesus."

"Inflame. Now, that sounds like the exact choice of evocative words needed to describe what happened up there."

Longarm sat upright in his seat. Ropy veins popped out on his neck. "Okay, okay. 'Pears as how I'm gonna be forced to relate exactly what transpired that infamous day. Lay out all the most minute details. Leastwise, them parts of the tale I didn't bother to include in my previous o-fficial report. Had hoped not to relive the sorry episode, but I can see you're just itchin' to hear it."

"'Bout by-God time, too. Always knew that account you turned in concerning the *incident* was quite probably the most amazing piece of fiction ever written by one of my subordinates."

A wounded, petulant look swept over Longarm's face. "How'd that dance get to be an *incident*? Hell, Billy, you didn't believe my report? Why, I'm cut to the quick."

"Well, let's just say the physical reality didn't quite match that piece of wildly creative writing you turned in."

"Physical reality?"

"Jesus Christ on a crutch, Custis, when Jim Ed Cobb got back to Denver, most of his clothes had been burned off. Can't remember ever havin' a returning prisoner that'd been set aflame. Damn near half the town of Le Beau burned to the ground as well. Remember? Seems you failed to include those two tiny bits of fairly enlightening information in that fantastic composition of yours. Artful piece of work Henry's got filed away in one of the cabinets out there next to his desk."

Longarm squirmed in his seat. "Ah. Well, okay then. If you just have to hear the tale from the horse's mouth, gonna tell it all. Here's what happened. Whole weasel, hair, teeth, and toenails. Won't include a rustler's dream in the entire yarn. Promise. Swear on my sainted mother's grave."

Vail licked the end of his ash-laden stogie, then rolled it back and forth between chubby fingers like a Chicago banker about to make the deal of a lifetime. "Don't leave anything out now."

Longarm held one hand aloft as though being sworn and about to testify in court. "Won't. My sacred oath. On my honor as a true gentleman."

"Uh-huh. Well, go on. Go on."

"See, happened like this. Tore into Le Beau about fifteen seconds behind ole Jim Ed. I 'uz slingin' dirt clods like a Kansas thrashin' machine. Ran him to ground at the local livery and blacksmith shop. He 'uz lookin' for a spot to put his animal up for the night. Stupid gomer didn't even know I 'uz after him. Thing I didn't realize, though, 'uz that the smithy and Jim Ed were somethin' akin to long lost family."

"Distant cousins perhaps."

"Yeah, maybe. Coulda been. Pair of 'em looked a lot alike. In a kinda face-like-hammered-horseshit way. Know what I mean? Anyhow, jumped off that jughead of mine at a dead run, had my hand on the grips of my pistol. Yelled for Jim Ed to grab the nearest cloud. Outta fuckin' nowhere this big son-of-a-bitch horseshoe-bendin' idiot popped up from behind a blazin' forge. Went to swingin' a three-foot-long red-hot brandin' iron at my head. 'Course, I feinted and ducked. And fortunately, he missed."

"Figured as much. Didn't notice any blistered, puss-filled, scab-covered dents in that thick West Virginia noggin of yours."

"Don't make me lose my train of thought, Billy. I'm on a roll here."

"Oh, sorry. I'll keep quiet. Please, do continue."

"Well, as I 'uz sayin', that smithy took a mighty swing at me. Lost his balance. Lard-gutted shit kicker went to twirlin' around like some kinda fat-assed ballet dancer. Spun and stumbled hisself right into a stack of hay next to the front door of his operation and fell down."

"Uh-oh. See where this is going already."

"Yeah. Sure 'nuff. Hot piece of iron he had in his hand set that heap of dried-out grass ablaze. Quicker'n you can snap your fingers, that pile of animal feed exploded in ten-foot-tall flames. In about as much time as it'd take a body to spit, whole front facade of his livery outfit was blazin' to beat the band. Building went up like a July Fourth whiz-bang. Damnest thing I ever saw. Couldn't do mucha nothin' but stand there with my mouth gaped open. Amazin'. Really amazin'."

"Incredible. Just incredible. But you still haven't told me how Jim Ed Cobb ended up on fire."

"I 'uz gettin to that. Trust me. Gotta picture the scene now. Smithy his very own self has accidentally set his place of business afire. He's hoppin' around, yelpin' like a wild Injun. Jim Ed and me are so stunned, we're just standin' there in the street few feet from each other, with our chins on our chests like gape-mouthed idiots."

"Pair of gape-mouthed idiots. Sounds about right."

"Yeah. Well, guess Jim Ed musta come outta his bout of

stupefacturated amazement quicker'n I did. Went for that meat cleaver of a bowie knife he favors."

"Amazing."

"Swear it's the truth. Started chasin' me around the smithy's forge. Hackin' and a-slashin' like some kinda fool the whole time. Put a buncha unwanted vents in my best suit jacket. Kept yellin' over my shoulder as how he'd best put that pigsticker down 'fore I got fed up with his shenanigans. Well, you can bet the ranch he didn't listen. So, 'bout my third or fourth trip 'round that forge, I got tired of the whole dance. Got a step or two ahead, stopped, turned around, and shot the ignorant bone-headed son of a bitch in the foot."

In spite of himself, Billy Vail let a huffing chuckle escape. Then he coughed into his hand, rearranged the papers on his desk, and tried to act as though nothing had happened.

"Well, by God, Billy, ole Jim Ed sure 'nuff dropped that big ole bowie. Went to grabbin' at his foot, howlin' and a-stumblin' backward toward that flamin' pile of silage. Couldn't latch onto 'im myself. And by then, his friend was addin' to all the confusion by runnin' in and out of the front entrance of his livery operation a-leadin' scared horses to safety. So, 'fore I can get a hand on Jim Ed and stop 'im from fallin' into the fire, he lurched over directly into that con-flag-ration like a red-eyed drunk. Fell right into the middle of it, Billy."

"Jim Ed fell into the fire."

"Well, yeah. Hell, yeah. Can you believe that? 'Course, he didn't stay there very long."

Vail slapped the arm of his chair. "Bet he didn't."

"No. Swear it. Hopped right up. Real quicklike. Back of his shirt, and maybe some of his pants, was just a-blazin'. Well, of course, he went to runnin' and hollerin'. Flew over to a local mercantile outfit not far from that livery business like a spark-slingin' ball from a Roman candle."

Vail shook his head. Puffed on his cigar and stared at the ceiling.

"Ran in the front door and out the back, Billy. Then he fell slap into a water trough. But he musta bumped into a dry goods rack or somethin' along the way."

"Oh, Jesus."

"Yeah. Set the whole damned store on fire. Place kinda exploded. Think maybe the flames hit a supply of coal oil. Hellacious thunderin' explosion. Damnedest thing I'd ever seen. Well, next to the livery goin' up like it done."

"Jim Ed Cobb, by his lonesome, set Le Beau's only mercantile store ablaze?"

"Yep. Sure as hell did."

"You're telling me that you had nothing to do with the ensuing inferno? Nothing at all?"

"Why, hell, no. The hay, the barn, the mercantile, none a that was my fault. Jesus, I 'uz just tryin' my best to arrest the crazy bastard and, hopefully, stay alive in the process. Wanna blame that mess on somebody, oughta put it all on that stupid, stumble-footed blacksmith."

"How about the Lone Wolf Saloon, across Le Beau's main thoroughfare from the mercantile store?"

Longarm took a nervous puff off his cigar, shook it at Billy Vail, then said, "Sparks, by God."

"Sparks?"

"Windier'n hell up on the Rattlesnake that day. So dry the local lizards had army canteens strapped on their little lizard backs. Mercantile store got to goin' good. Stiff breeze carried a sheet of hissin' embers across the street. Lone Wolf went up like a barrel of firecrackers."

"And the town's only functioning café?"

"Well, now, unfortunately, Coker's Café was located hard by the Lone Wolf. Couldn't a been more'n a foot of open space 'tween them two buildings. No alley. So close, in fact, once that waterin' hole got goin' good, café next door didn't stand any more chance'n a longhorn steer in a

Chicago packin' plant. Both of 'em burned slap to the ground."

Billy Vail let out an exasperated sigh, then placed his head in his hands and groaned. "So, you're telling me that inside of ten minutes of your arrival, nigh on half the established businesses of the tiny hamlet of Le Beau, Wyoming Territory, went up in flames?"

"Yeah. And weren't a single, cracklin' stick of wood of it my fault. 'Less you wanna somehow claim that by shootin' Jim Ed Cobb in the foot I was the cause of the subsequent, catastrophic firestorm. Be quite a stretch in court, though, I'd imagine."

Vail's assistant strolled into the office and dropped a thick envelope in Longarm's lap. "Best get a rush on, Deputy Marshal Long," he said. "Your train leaves in less than two hours."

Longarm struggled out of the chair, then stuffed his hat back on. He held the manila package up and knifed a gaze at his boss. "Gonna even tell me who am I going out after this time, Billy? Could be of some help, you know."

For several seconds, the astonished and somewhat puzzled-looking U.S. marshal stared into space as though still totally dumbfounded by the tale of fiery insanity he'd just sat through. Finally, he leaned back in his chair and muttered, "Belly slinker name of Charlie Bugg. Know 'im?"

"Sure. I know ole Charlie. He's a bad one. Not nearly as bad as his younger brother, Jennings, but bad enough. What'd he do?"

"Know both men on sight?"

"'Course I do. Bit better acquainted with Jennings, being as how we've had our differences in the past. Already arrested him a time or two. Some of their nearest and dearest compadres are as bad, or worse than either of them Bugg boys, when you really get to thinkin' on it, Billy. But to put a fine point on your question, yeah, I could pick either man out of a crowd. 'Less they were hidin' themselves amidst a pack of hairy, puckered-up assholes. Then I might have to really look for 'em."

"Well, Charlie and some of his amigos robbed an east-bound C.B. & Q. express car filled with currency and coin. Hit 'em over close to Wiggins. Money was on its way back East from the mint. Killed a couple of special deputies assigned to guard the shipment in the process. Copy of the entire report's inside that package. Read it and you'll know as much as I do."

Longarm fingered his sheaf of papers, then said, "Jennings ridin' with Charlie on this raid?"

Vail shook his head. "Can't say for sure at the moment. Nobody's mentioned his name, leastways not so far. Only have a single witness that was able to identify Charlie, and he's been shot up pretty good. Past that, rest of our information is a bit on the sketchy side, to say the very least. Figure most of the witnesses are too afraid to say one way or the other."

"But you're certain Charlie's in Fort Stockton right now?"

Vail nodded as he traced one-fingered circles in a patch of dust covering the only open spot atop his desk. "According to the most creditable report we have available at the moment—maybe. My best hunch is that he's headed south and east from there by now. Way I've got it figured, you should catch the murdering bastard somewhere between Fort Stockton and Eagle Pass. That is, if you get a move on, catch your train, and really kick hard for the border once you get to Stockton. Information we've developed indicates those Bugg boys have family in Eagle Pass. Bunch of idiot cousins livin' there most likely. Given the need for help and assistance after committing such a crime, know it's the direction I'd take if I were Charlie Bugg."

Longarm turned on his heel and headed for the door. Over his shoulder, he called out, "I'm on it, Boss. Have this sack of evil scum back here for trial, or dead, quick as I can."

When Billy Vail heard the outer door slam shut behind his deputy, he leaned back in his chair and said, "Think I'd like to be left alone for a few minutes, Henry."

A concerned look etched its way across the anxious secretary's face. "Are you all right, Marshal Vail?"

"Yeah. Leastwise, I think so. Just give me a few peaceful minutes, Henry. Need time to digest Deputy Marshal Long's yarn of fire, foot-shot bandits, burning saloons, and irate, soot-covered Wyoming citizens I just heard. Might even want to try and keep anyone else out of my office for at least an hour or two. Especially that band of idiot senators. Whatever else you do for the next hour or so, keep them the hell outta here."

"Do my best, sir."

"Right now, my brain hurts. Feels like somebody just hit me in the head with an ax. And given my distress at the moment, wouldn't want to shoot anyone bold enough to add to my problems."

Vail's administrative assistant turned and tiptoed back toward his own office. At his boss's door, and just before he gently pulled the portal closed, Henry heard the marshal moan, "Sweet Merciful Jesus."

Chapter 3

"Well, Sneezer, ain't this the most amazing piece of luck we've had on this godforsaken trip?" Custis Long patted his drooping, sweat-soaked animal on the neck, then urged it forward.

A blisteringly hot sun the color of molten lead baked the back of the weary deputy marshal's neck as he steered the Fort Stockton remount to a rough-hewn hitch rail beneath the only shade tree on the entire, rutted, dusty street. Limp-leafed live oak stood out front of a coarse-looking joint named the Lame Dog Saloon.

Horse-weary, the near-worn-out, saddle-sore lawman eased off the tired bay gelding's back. He flipped the reins over the tie-up's rude, uneven top railing, but didn't bother to lash them down.

Hands on hips, Longarm groaned, then bent over at the waist in an attempt to stretch trail-kinked back and leg muscles. Grindingly slow, he came erect again while running gritty hands along the backs of knotted thighs. He briefly massaged sore tendons, ligaments, and sinew that ached as though someone had beaten him silly with a petrified tree limb. A spot just above the base of his spine felt as though the horse had stepped on him during the night.

"Sweet sufferin' Virginia. Hard for me to decide which is worse," he said to the horse on finally attaining his full height again. "Ridin' the rails from Denver to Nowhere, Texas, while perched on one a them damned rock-hard day coach benches, or havin' to sit on your ass-bustin' back for damn nigh on two hundred hot, ball-bustin' miles."

The horse blinked fatigue-laden eyes at the yammering, rambling lawman, then shoved its muzzle into the life-replenishing liquid in the trough at its feet.

"Few more years of this shit," Longarm continued to no one in particular, "swear 'fore Jesus I'll likely be a hobbling, shuffle-butted cripple. Be livin' in some snake pit of a home for the elderly and half-witted. Probably shoulda stopped in Sonora or Val Verde for a restful night in a bed."

He leaned as far back as he could without tipping over like a kid's toy top. "Sleepin' on the ground with spiders, scorpions, and snakes sure as hell don't help none, that's for damn certain," he mumbled to himself.

The inscrutable Sneezer snapped his dripping muzzle out of the water trough. The sturdy gelding snorted, then shook his black-maned equine head. Misty beads of liquid flew from soaked lips. Animal twisted a finely shaped neck and cast a sad-eyed gaze at the grumbling lawman, as though he understood every word Longarm had uttered.

The sweat-and-froth-drenched beast switched its dust-powdered ebon tail, then stamped a back foot—a vain, halfhearted attempt at shooing the biting, thumb-sized flies away from his massive rump. He rattled the braided-hair bridle and metal bit, then went back to the revitalizing water in the trough. Muscles beneath the animal's reddish yellow hair twitched and quivered as the enormous flying insects buzzing around his behind shifted their assault to areas less accessible to a switching tail or knifelike hooves.

With one hand pressed to a spot on a knotted lower spine just above his pistol belt, Longarm stepped onto the boardwalk beneath the Lame Dog Saloon's sheltering, shade-giving veranda. He turned, gritted his teeth, then cast a wary, unhurried, professional glance from one end of

Buckhorn's short, wind-blown main thoroughfare to the other.

Here and there along the nearly abandoned street, a few other heat-weary hay burners stood tethered in front of a tired-looking general mercantile store, a café with a weather-blasted sign out front that designated it as Wilson's, and a dry goods concern named Overbee's. Pair of fine-looking pinto ponies drooped in the heat outside what appeared to be Buckhorn's only billiards parlor. And a sleek, well-fed chestnut sagged under the sun's unrelenting assault near the local marshal's office and jail.

Longarm spotted at least two other saloons farther down the deserted street, but neither appeared operational. Windows of a joint called the Empty Bucket were completely boarded over. And the Jumping Bean manifested the outward show of being inhabited by the ghosts of imbibers left over from some better years of the misty past.

A wave of boiling air rolled down the street from the west and swept over the weary lawman. Longarm recoiled as though someone had slapped him across his handsome, tanned face. He wiped a dripping chin on an already sweat-saturated shirt sleeve.

"Sure as the devil ain't much left of this burg," he mumbled under his breath. "Heavy blow outta Mexico comes along, bet this whole place vanishes like spit on a Montana stove lid in January. Ten years from now, it'll look like the earth just opened up and took it all back. Nothin' left but mesquite bushes and bleached bones."

The dust-blanketed deputy marshal beat at himself with his hat, then pushed through a set of wind-blistered batwing doors that hadn't seen a fresh coat of paint in at least twenty years. Rusted hinges groaned and squawked like a tied cat being tortured with a sharp stick. He drew to a halt barely two steps inside the cow country watering hole's front entrance. He let his vision adjust to the diminished light. The blistering heat eased somewhat in the cooler confines of the high-ceilinged, darkened saloon. Temperature eased a little, but not a hell of a lot.

To Longarm's dumbfounded amazement, the fanciest mahogany bar he'd ever encountered in such an out-of-the-way place ran the length of the building on his immediate right. Mirrors covered the wall behind the marble-topped serving station and highlighted a well-stocked back bar. The brass foot rail and all the spittoons he could lay an eye on sparkled, as though just shined a few minutes before his arrival. Four spotless felt-covered but unused poker tables sprouted from the floor on his left. The vacant chairs at each table gathered like wind-seared flower petals around a brilliant green center. Fine-looking snooker and pool tables inhabited the space on the opposite end of the room.

In the only nod toward something like ornamental embellishment, all the free wall space above heavily scarred wainscoting sported an astonishing array of oil paintings, printed representations, and sepia-toned photographs of naked females. Near a hundred images of various sizes and shapes, depicting women in all manner of seductive poses, covered virtually every inch of the entire partition.

Well, Longarm thought, if this amazing display of pulchritude don't draw customers in, nothing else will. The grinning lawdog tried to recall the last time he'd seen that many uncovered nipples in a single viewing.

The Lame Dog's biggest surprise of all, though, was four brass-embellished ceiling fans. Connected to one another by a bewildering series of leather belts, straps, and drive rods, they dangled from long brass poles like a string of glittering windmills. Even a Sonoran desert Gila monster would've found it grudgingly necessary to acknowledge that the hardly detectable but greatly appreciated agitation of West Texas's sweltering, stagnant air felt damned great.

A rustling flurry of activity at the far end of the saloon's immaculate slab of polished marble drew Longarm's attention to a grinning, friendly-looking drink slinger. Well-fed gent hopped off a stool topped with a gob of thick padding, then rushed in the thirsty lawman's direction. He swabbed a spot atop the flawless, glistening slab of stone with a damp piece of rag and said, "Just be kiss my own ass, a newly arrived, honest-to-God customer. Come right in, sir. Belly on up to my fine granite-topped bar. Damned good to see somebody. Hell, this time of day, damned good to see anybody for that matter. Beginnin' to feel most like I 'uz the only livin' man left in this part of the civilized world. If you can call this part of Tejas civilized."

Longarm eased up to the Lame Dog's liquor dispensing counter, then placed a booted foot on the brass rail. Tired to the bone, he leaned on both elbows and said, "Hope like hell you've got ice cold beer back there somewhere, friend."

The fat-bellied drink wrangler flashed a brilliantly polished pair of gold teeth glistening from the top centermost spot of his mouth. Man's sparkling smile looked like the sun coming up on a clear, cool morning.

"Oh, yes, sir," the jovial drink slinger said. "Can plainly see you're not a man prone to drink Extract of Old Bob Wire, or Essence of Rattlesnake Spit." Then he hurried back in the direction he'd originally come from. "Cold one on the way," he called over his shoulder. A few seconds later, he returned from the far end of the bar with a colossal-sized clear glass mug filled to overflowing with frosty, amber-colored wonderfulness. Slid it into Longarm's waiting hand.

"Cain't get any better'n this, 'less you wanna go all the way to San Angelo, amigo. And, best of all, 'at 'ere mug of frigid goodness is only twenty-five cents. Helluva deal no matter how you slice it."

Longarm put the glass to anxious lips and sucked half the chilled liquid down before he carefully set the container back onto the bar. Of a sudden, almost as though a miracle had occurred, the worn-to-a-frazzle lawman felt rejuvenated.

Foamy suds decorated the handlebar mustache above his grinning lips when he ran a sleeve across his beer-dampened mouth and chin, then said, "God Almighty, but I needed that, *mi amigo gordo*. You just can't imagine how much. Walked in here feelin' like a catfish covered with a buncha blood-suckin' Alabama dog ticks. Gotta say them fans of yours helped some, but gloriosity, this here beer brought on the magic."

The barman's radiant, golden, break-of-day grin grew ever wider. He winked, flicked a finger heavenward. "Got a Messican in back what pedals the contraption that keeps the blades a-movin' and a-stirrin' the air around. Sure 'nuff helps with this near-unbearable heat." He reached across the bar's polished slab of marble and offered a hand the size of a camp skillet. "Name's Spider Troop, stranger. Good to have you stop in, sir. Mighty good."

Longarm shook the big man's hand, then said, "Custis Long, Spider. You lived around this area any length of time?"

"Been watchin' the sun come up in the dyin' metropolis of Buckhorn near ten years, Custis."

"I see."

"Know exactly how you feel 'bout now, my friend. Felt the same way when I first arrived. This time of year, it's hotter'n a burnin' stump 'round these parts. Feller walks down the street and he'll get blisters on his boot heels 'fore he can get from one end to the other."

Longarm grinned, then took another sip of his foam-topped gulp-and-shudder juice.

Troop was on a roll and kept going. "Ole desert rat buddy a mine, who comes in here almost every afternoon 'bout this time, says as how our particular part of Texas makes hell look like a St. Louis icehouse. Hotter outside than the town square down in Nuevo Laredo durin' fiesta time. Makes me gladder'n hell the feller what built this place installed these fans, tell you for damn sure."

Before Longarm could take another much-needed swig from his sweating glass, the Lame Dog's drink shuffler snatched the mug away and waddled toward the far end of the bar again. "Lemme freshen 'er up for you there, Custis. Make 'er nice and icy cold again. Get a frosty mug a this heavenly ambrosia just right and you'll come down with one a them brain-freeze sessions. Be grabbin' your head and moanin' like a virgin what just got a hole punched in 'er."

For the next few minutes, Longarm nursed his sudsy, dripping drink and listened while the gold-toothed Spider Troop rattled on about everything from the vagaries of weather to poisonous desert critters, to local history, Texas politics, national politics, and finally, the price of beef cattle in Kansas City. Took but a few minutes for Longarm to realize that the good-humored saloon owner appeared totally entranced by the sound of his own voice.

An inch or so from the bottom of his second mug, Longarm waved the talkative whiskey wrangler into silence and said, "'S all very interesting, but you by any chance ever have a piece of murderous trash named Charlie Bugg come in here for a froth-topped, cold libation like this 'un, Spider?"

For the first time, Troop's affable smile bled away. One eyebrow arched almost all the way up into his hairline. He nervously wiped the same spot at least three times and swayed back and forth like a confused, gold-toothed grizzly bear.

Longarm carefully eyeballed Troop, then said, "Can't miss the man. Has a real nasty scar runnin' down the right side of his ass-ugly face. Looks almost like somebody tried to take his head off with a hay hook."

Troop ran his damp chunk of frayed rag from forehead to sweat-covered chin, then, as though in pain, nodded. Man near whispered when he leaned over the bar, motioned for Longarm to move closer, and said, "Evil son of a bitch that Bugg feller, Custis. Hate to see him comin' through my door, but 'pears as how he likes my fans and beer same as you. Few customers I have left these days usually take a hike soon's he shows that repulsive kisser of his. 'Course, that always depends on just how bad they want a cold one. Man wantin' a brew like one a these a mine'll put up with just about anything, even a walking, hair-covered asshole like Charlie Bugg. 'Sides, I'm the only place left in town where a body can get a drink these days."

Longarm grinned, then twirled his mug around in the wet ring beneath the sweating glass. "Charlie make an appearance often?"

Troop set to wiping everything in sight, as though he didn't particularly cotton to continuing the conversation. He shot quick, darting glances around the barren room, then over Longarm's shoulder toward the Lame Dog's sun drenched front entrance.

"Mad-dog mean son of a bitch stops in for a visit way too regular to suit my taste," Troop said. "Worst of it's that he's pretty consistent in his habits. Usually already been around by now. Truth be told, cain't say for sure why he ain't come in for his daily bout of bottomless consumption yet. 'Course, it could be the weather. Gets hotter'n election day in a yellow jacket nest, like it is now, folks tend to stay inside, you know. Ain't prone to move around much. But ole Charlie's kinda like a fat pig in a mud waller, don't seem to be bothered much by the heat. Comes sniffin' 'round no matter how hot it gets. Man snorts up enough liquor in a day's time to fill half a dozen armadiller holes."

"Regular customer, huh?"

"Been close to drunker'n a hoedown fiddler ever since he hit town near'bouts a month ago."

"Ah. That a fact? Livin' somewhere nearby?"

"Spends his nights down on the far end of Main Street in the Nueces House. Barely passable five-room casa the owner, Alfonso Perez, claims as a hotel. Charlie rents a half-furnished room there. Figure the only reason he stays in the place's 'cause, for them as request it, Alfonso can get a feller a hot-to-trot señorita—for the right monetary consideration, a course."

Longarm nodded and continued to nip at the dwindling, frosty liquid in his glass.

"Way I hear the story," Troop said, "Bugg's Alfonso's only payin' customer at present. Think there mighta been several other men layin' over when the evil bastard arrived in town. But he run 'em all off in a matter of days."

"Well, he's always been a hard case. Tougher'n keeping a mountain lion under a washtub to get along with, from all observable past indications."

"Ain't that the truth. Tale goin' 'round town is that he likes to lay up on his meaner'n-hell ass all night with two, three, sometimes four women at a pop. Man must have the constitution of a range-crazed bull, and a bag of gold coin the size of the back boot on a Concord coach."

Still propped on his elbows, Longarm took another long swig of the conversation-inducing jig juice, then flashed a friendly grin. "Say he ran all 'em other fellers stayin' in the hotel off? How'd he manage that?"

"Easy. Pistol-whipped the dog shit outta one unfortunate son of Texas. Poor feller objected to all the racket comin' outta Bugg's room of a night. Drummer who liked to put up in Alfonso's place when he was workin' his route 'tween Fort Stockton and San Angelo. Evil skunk Bugg caught the unsuspectin' man next mornin' and done the job right in Alfonso's closet-sized lobby."

"Sweet Virginia. Pistol-whipped the man in the hotel lobby? Ole Bugg's a hard case all right."

"Damn straight. Some of the hotel's other patrons seen the sorry deed take place. Rest of 'em heard 'bout it right quick after the uncalled-for bloodlettin'. Whole bunch checked out faster'n jackrabbits with their tails on fire. Ever one of 'em headed the hell outta Buckhorn pretty damned quick after that. Least, that's the way I heard the story."

Longarm gazed at the reflected image of the batwing entryway in the spotless polished mirror along the wall. He sipped his drink, carefully placed the mug in the same damp spot, then said, "On the way into town, noticed a marshal's office down the street a piece, Spider. Your lawman try to do anything about Charlie? Maybe correct his errant behavior?"

Troop flipped his raggedy towel onto one beefy shoulder, gritted shiny metal teeth, then placed both hands atop the bar and spread stubby fingers. "Tell the God's truth, Custis, we ain't got a for-real marshal no more."

"You're kiddin'."

"Nope. Man quit and hoofed it outta town 'bout a year ago. Left us with a sorry-assed piece of a deputy name of Jesse Klegg. Man's 'bout as worthless as gettin' a haircut on nothin' but the middle part of your head. Get it? Absolutely good for nothin', that's what he is. On top of everthang else, he's ugly. Son of a bitch looks like one a them Mexican fruit bats. Just 'bout everyone in town agrees as how Bugg scared Jesse near shitless with that pistol-whippin' business. Personally doubt our gutless town deputy would even venture outta the jailhouse—lest it was burnin' slap down 'round his rather sizable, hair-covered, pointy ears."

"Charlie Bugg's behavior got anything to do with the fact that there's hardly anyone to be seen on the street, Spider? You could fire a howitzer from one end of the sunbaked main thoroughfare to the other and not hit a living soul."

Troop looked puzzled for about a second, then said, "Well, maybe. But, hell, Custis, anybody what ain't totally blind can see that the town of Buckhorn's on its last leg. Place is, for damned certain, gonna be a ghost town in a few years."

"Yeah, noticed that myself soon as I rode in. Saw several other liquor lockers on down the street that looked like they'd already bit the dust."

"Uh-huh. Lame Dog's the only functionin' place to get a decent drink left in town. Okay by me, but honest to God, if'n I could find a half-brained idiot buyer for this place, I'd be on my way to El Paso, Fort Worth, or Dallas faster'n a turpentined cat. But, shit, looks like I'm gonna have to ride this nag till it falls down and dies an ugly death. 'Bout the only thing keeps me goin' is a daily afternoon gatherin' of locals who come by to visit and have a snort or two. Friends and business acquaintances from hereabouts, you know."

Longarm glanced into the mirror again, then said, "'Course. Understand completely. Say Charlie usually comes in pert regular, huh?"

"Yep. Troublemakin' bastard's one of my handful of payin' customers. Don't like the son of a bitch—not even the least little bit. He's one angry, abusive, cantankerous pain in the ass. Threatens to kick my behind so hard I'll have to loosen my collar to take a dump damn nigh every time he walks through my swingin' doors. But, like I said before, he does pay. Makin' his way all over town spendin' spankin'-new gold coins like pourin' water outten a boot, as a matter of pure fact."

Longarm's brows knitted beneath the canyonlike creases across a deeply tanned forehead. His steely-eyed gaze narrowed. He pursed chapped lips, then said, "Do tell. You still got any of 'em?"

"Sure do. Been hoardin' up all he's willin' to part with."

"Got one handy you can show me?"

Troop nodded, took several steps back toward his corner stool, fumbled around beneath the bar, then rolled a sparkling new double-eagle gold piece in Longarm's direction. The inquisitive lawman snatched the coin up and gave it a careful eyeballing. Flipped it into the air and listened as it bounced off the marble.

Troop flashed a big crooked grin. "Thing of beauty, ain't she? Ever time I look at one of 'em reminds me of my own teeth, don'cha know. Just fuckin' love the way they jingle when one of 'em hits this piece of stone."

"Yeah. Beautiful. And best of all, it's the real deal," Longarm said, and rolled the coin back. "Freshly minted. Don't get much newer'n one like this. Charlie got a bunch of 'em when he and four or five other desperadoes robbed an eastbound Union Pacific express car outta Denver 'bout two months ago. Near as can be determined, them boys took near half a million dollars worth of gold coin and paper money. Coins were all brothers and sisters of this one."

"Musta been one helluva load."

"Still trying to figure out exactly how they pulled it off. Complicated raid. Involved stopping a Chicago, Burlington & Quincy train, breakin' into a heavily armored and guarded railcar, then loadin' the loot into at least one wagon. Maybe several. More important than their methods, though, they went and killed two deputy U.S. marshals that were ridin' guard. 'S why I'm here. Figure on takin' Ole Charlie back to Denver for suitable trial and a righteous hanging. Or, done made up my mind, I'll kill him if he's otherwise inclined. Either way, Buckhorn won't have to put up with the evil skunk too much longer."

Spider Troop's metallic grin sparkled. "Figured you for a lawdog soon's you stepped across my threshold. Can spot you fellers from a hundred yards away. Just somethin' 'bout how you carry yourselves. Got that hard-eyed look of a dangerous man. All confidence and deadly, coiled-up action just waitin' to spring loose."

Longarm flashed a self-conscious grin. "Well, if that's what you saw when I walked in, Spider, it's a total surprise to me. Don't see much like that when I look in the mirror to shave. Think maybe you've been readin' way too many of them penny dreadfuls."

"Well, hell, what else's a man gonna do when he's stuck in an environment like this 'un?"

"Understand. But you surely must realize that consumption of the printed delusional bullshit by the authors of those rags could well cause the most practical man to fall into fits of thinkin' as how them as follow a career in the law are gifted with talents that might not exist."

Troop shuffled around behind his elaborate bar and grinned like a kid who'd just got caught with his hands in the neighbor girl's knickers. "True enough, I suppose. But still and all, have to stick with my original assessment. Just knew you 'uz a badge toter soon's you strolled in."

Longarm pushed his mug across the bar. "I defer to your hidden talents as a seer, Spider. Why don't you fill 'er up again. Think I'll take a seat in the corner yonder. Looks right peaceful over there. Kinda dark, shadowy, outta the way. Rest my saddle-sore back a bit. Maybe pull my hat down over my eyes and indulge in a much-needed siesta. Stick around for a spell and see if ole Charlie shows his ugly kisser."

Spider Troop shoved Longarm's refreshed glass down the bar, grinned, then said, "Doubt you could find a quieter place in Buckhorn if you looked all day, Marshal Long. That skunk Charlie comes in, you'll know it. As you're well aware, the man's an incurable loudmouth and chronic troublemaker."

Chapter 4

In a matter of minutes after Longarm's saddle-bruised behind hit the corner chair he'd picked, the run-down, run-over, and wrung-out lawdog had involuntarily nodded off into a restful catnap. The blue black hole of much-needed rest opened up beneath Spider Troop's felt-covered corner table. Longarm's eyes drooped, his chin dropped to his chest, and he jumped into the yawning chasm of sleep with both dusty booted feet.

The energy-sapping warmth of the day, just enough ice-cold beer, and an abiding need for a relaxing breather soon had the bone-tired lawman deep into the kind of raunchy reverie usually reserved for nights draped over a lumpy hotel mattress. Dreamy visions of a high-breasted, pert-nippled, blond-haired beauty of his acquaintance who lived on the outskirts of Trinidad flickered across the backs of his fluttering, sleep-heavy eyelids.

About the time the drowsing deputy marshal had managed to get the cobalt-eyed Hattie McDonald buck-assed naked and bouncing up and down on his steely prong in his drowsing fantasy, Longarm was snapped back to groggy-brained consciousness. The noisy eruption of angry voices, barely a dozen feet away from his quiet corner nest, snatched him out of Hattie's talented cooch and deposited the bleary-eyed lawman back in the real world of mind-numbing Texas heat.

"Shit," he mumbled, then ran a hand across quick-blinking eyes.

A shake of the head got rid of most of Longarm's sleep-induced cobwebs and revealed a scene much different from the one he'd abandoned by falling asleep. For reasons unfathomable to a half-conscious visitor's unpracticed eye, the Lame Dog Saloon had perked up considerably during what had seemed a very short siesta. Once his fog-blurred mind cleared a bit more, Longarm realized that Spider Troop's favorite perambulating booze-and-bullshit crowd had quietly gathered during his much-needed nap and was huffing along full tilt in spite of the stifling heat.

Nearly half a dozen newly arrived patrons now took up room at the bar. An equal number of others had seats at all the previously empty tables. Typical small town meet-and-drink session on tap every afternoon at about the same time. The exact daily ritual Troop had so precisely described earlier, the awakening lawman thought. A simple chance for men of various social stations, who'd likely have known each other for years, to meet, socialize, and unwind.

Longarm rubbed one eye with the cracked knuckle of his hand, checked the time with his Ingersoll watch, and couldn't believe what he saw. He'd been asleep for almost two hours. He shoved the big-ticking timepiece back into his vest pocket. Fired a rum-soaked nickel cheroot and watched Charlie Bugg sway back and forth on unsteady feet at the bar. The scar-faced villain had one of the lately-on-the-scene local imbibers by the collar and was slapping the bejabberous hell out of the unfortunate fellow.

"Man what looks at me the wrong way can expect to get his ears boxed, mister," Bugg shouted, loud enough to be heard at the other end of Buckhorn's only street. Then he twisted hell out of the wretched-looking man's collar, and smacked him so hard across his already blistered cheek, it knocked the smaller chap's wire-framed glasses onto the dust-covered floor.

The once-bespectacled gent getting his face whacked stood nigh on a head and a half shorter than Bugg, and appeared on the verge of total, panicked collapse. Hands upturned in the classic gesture of one trying to pacify a hard-hearted brute, he cried out, "Assure you, sir, I meant no offense. None at all. Please, please, don't strike me any more."

Bugg jerked the smaller man erect and belted him again. Open-palmed rap to the cheek sounded like a pistol shot. A thin stream of bright red blood trickled from the corner of the abused man's trembling mouth. Along with all the confusion and embarrassment, the poor wretch on the receiving end of the ill treatment found himself decorated with a glowing, scarlet handprint on either side of his overheated face. Specks of blood decorated his brilliantly white dress shirt.

Seated at the table closest to the Lame Dog's café doors, a silver-haired, dignified-looking gentleman decked out in the typical attire of a well-heeled banker shook an accusatory finger in Charlie Bugg's direction and boldly called out, "No need for that kind of crude behavior, Mr. Bugg. I'm absolutely certain Horace meant you no ill will by accidentally casting an unguarded glance in the direction of your grandiose personage. Besides, taking offense at a wayward glance is, by any standard, an idiotic response. Why don't you go back to your drinking and leave the poor man alone." Under his breath, the gent added, "You insufferable wretch."

Longarm immediately admired the silver-haired gent's gritty nerve, and wondered how any man of conscience could have acted otherwise. He smiled, then covered his lips with one hand. Surreptitiously, he continued to watch as the dangerous, festering scene of uncalled-for violence continued to unfold.

A sneering Charlie Bugg pushed the object of his assault backward, then turned toward the silver-haired man at the table. His rheumy-eyed gaze leisurely swept away from poor red-cheeked Horace, and drew a derisive bead on the man who looked like a banker. "Well, now, Horace, 'pears as how you done went and got one a Buckhorn's foremost citizens stickin' up fer ya. How's zat make you feel, you weasel-faced stack of steamin' shit. Richest of the entire town's citizens has gone and nerved up and's a-takin' your part."

Bugg's angry, arch-browed glare narrowed on the silver-haired man like the sights on a Sharps Big .50. "Tell you what, Mr. Bankerman Ben Tucker," he growled, "bein' as how you're so fuckin' high-and-mighty 'round these god-forsaken parts, why don't you get on outta that chair. Come right up here to the bar and *make me* quit doin' the kinda thang I've always found right entertainin'."

Without even looking in the recently slapped, red-faced fellow's direction, Bugg's arm snaked out and delivered another stunning rap across the mouth of the object of his insensitive bullying. Then he seized the smaller man by the shoulders and shook him. "Warms my ice-covered heart anytime I can spend a few minutes embarrassin' hell out of a pocket-sized little chicken shit like ole Horace here." Bugg grabbed the hapless Horace's cheek between a thumb and forefinger, and pinched the poor man until he squealed like a stuck pig.

The gent Bugg had referred to as Tucker waved the angry challenge aside with a well-manicured hand wrapped around a half-full glass of rye. As though dismissively swatting at a worrisome cockroach, he said, "Like most bullying trash of your type, sir, you grossly overestimate your importance in the scheme of things. Your *kind* seems to always have insectlike antenna out for the most mundane of offenses. Perhaps more importantly, though, even a fool as stupid as you are should know that I would never bother to dirty my hands with scum like you, Bugg. I'd hire the job out to your betters."

Charlie Bugg's unshaven face reddened and went slack. He flipped the hammer thong off the Colt's pistol at his hip, then let his hand rest on the weapon's yellowed, carved-bone grip. An ugly, mocking sneer played across cruel lips when he said, "Like I told you before, oh, high-and-mighty Tucker, don't like the way I care to amuse myself, why don't you just get on up outten that chair and make me stop, you mealy-mouthed, money-grubbin' son of a bitch."

The gallant Tucker didn't back off. He met Charlie Bugg's hot-eyed challenge with an icy stare as cold as an Idaho outhouse seat in January. "You've had way more than enough room to do as you please ever since arriving in Buckhorn, Mr. Bugg. But now, the good folks of my town have grown decidedly weary of you and your violent behavior. So, here's some heartfelt advice. Don't make me go to the telegraph office and send for someone who'll squash you like the crawling, slime-spreading pest you are."

Bugg belched like an overfed dog. A wave of hot bile brought a livid flush to his already glowing countenance. His chapped, purple lips twitched. Thumb-sized slobbers dribbled down his chin when he snarled, "Got-damned good chance you won't make it to them swingin' doors, you prissy-assed cocksucker. Much less Buckhorn's fuckin' telegraph office."

Tucker smiled. He leisurely took another sip from his drink. Placed the near-empty glass on the table, then pulled a penknife from his vest pocket and started cleaning already immaculate fingernails. The dismissive display appeared to infuriate the bleary-eyed outlaw at the bar.

As though talking to a headstrong child, Tucker pushed back in his chair, then said, "So, you intend to kill an unarmed man right in front of all these witnesses. Commit the murder of a defenseless man while a dozen onlookers stand by and watch. That the case, Mr. Bugg?"

Longarm came nigh on laughing out loud, but he realized that banker Tucker might well have gone too far, and figured it was about time to intervene before someone got badly hurt or, worse, seriously dead.

He slipped sweat-dampened fingers around the grips of his double-action Colt .44 Lightning, then kicked the empty chair nearest him toward the mouthy back-shooter at the bar. The heavy-bottomed wooden seat skittered and squawked across the uneven saloon's floorboards, ricocheted off Bugg's leg, and flipped onto its side with a resounding thump.

Only a few of the stunned attendees grouped at the Lame Dog's marble-topped liquor counter near the surprised Bugg heard it when Longarm hissed, "That's way more'n plenty outta you, Charlie. Ask me, you've gone and made a big enough horse's ass out of yourself for one day. Time to give that gusher of a mouth of yours a much-needed rest. 'Sides, way I see it, you get Mr. Tucker onto your three-times-more'n-ugly ass, you might not live out the week."

Like the twin barrels of a twelve-gauge Greener loaded with heavy-gauge buckshot, Bugg's bloodshot, hot-eyed gaze swiveled in Longarm's direction. Man had the look of complete disbelief stamped across his twisted, scarred countenance. "Got a lotta got-damned nerve kickin' a chair into me, you stringy asshole. Then exposin' yerself as some kinda mouthy son of a bitch what's lookin' to get squished like a festered pimple."

Longarm tapped the ivory grip of his pistol with a single fingernail. Everyone standing anywhere near Bugg moved as far away from the man as they could get and still bear amused witness to whatever bloodshed might be afoot.

Spider Troop retreated so far back into his favorite corner, he virtually vanished. Unfortunate red-cheeked Horace headed for the batwings. But he drew to a halt just inside the entryway, then backed up against the door frame and turned sidewise for a better view of the coming action. The unspoken hope that Charlie Bugg was about to die, gut-shot and crying out for his mother, flashed across the little man's face as clearly as if he'd screamed it loud enough for winged angels guarding the Pearly Gates to hear.

Longarm flashed a toothy, mocking grin in Charlie Bugg's direction. "Way I hear it, you ain't never been much of a gunhand, Charlie. Might have these folks buffaloed, but that don't mean a sack of dog shit to me. Besides, you're so drunk right now, you couldn't hit your own ass with a set of moose antlers and ten free jabs. Go to pullin' that hogleg and you're likely to shoot yourself in *both* feet. On top of all that, you're not jawin' at one of the local hoople-heads anymore."

"Oh, yeah? Well, just who'n the hell are you, mister?"

"Deputy U.S. marshal workin' out of Denver. Have an officially sworn warrant in my saddlebags for your immediate arrest. Seems you and a number of your closest friends went and robbed the federal government of some freshly minted gold coin and recently printed paper money. Right considerable amount, as a matter of pure fact. Killed two of my fellow law enforcement officers in the process. A man just can't go around doing idiotic shit like that. Government takes a mighty dim view of such behavior. Sends professionals like me out when you do. Shoulda figured it by now. I'm the living, breathing embodiment of your worst nightmare, Charlie."

A puzzled, panicky look momentarily flicked across Bugg's face. "Professionals like you, huh? My worst fuckin' nightmare, no damned less. So, what the hell's that mean? Man this far away from real civilization can claim anythang he can lay a lyin' tongue on. Declare as how you're the law. Well, I cain't see it. Just how'n the hell'er you any different than these other shit kickers here."

With all the unhurried, icy deliberation of a diamondback rattler eyeing a juicy jackrabbit supper, Longarm slowly rose from his seat. His right hand never left the age-yellowed grip of the cross-draw pistol strapped high on his left side. "Because, Charlie," Longarm growled, "if you nerve up enough to lift that hogleg so much as a quarter of an inch out of its holster, unlike any of these fine gents, I'll kill the hell outta you right where you stand."

Bugg blanched as though he'd been slapped.

"You'll be dead before you hit the floor, Charlie. All these gents as give a royal shit will be attending your funeral tomorrow. Or then again, bein' as how you're such an arrogant, dim-witted churnhead, maybe not."

One of Bugg's eyes uncontrollably blinked. A muscle in his jaw twitched. "That a fact," he grunted. "You got a name by any chance, Mr. Professional Gunman and Lawdog?"

Longarm grinned. "Custis Long. Deputy U.S. Marshal Custis Long. My friends, and most of my enemies, often call me Longarm."

Though transitory, a fleeting look of stunned recognition appeared to flash somewhere behind Bugg's eyes. "Longarm?" he muttered. "Well, by God, ain't that a caution. Admit I've heard the name before. Yeah, heard plenty 'bout you. Bad news all the way around. If you're actually who you claim."

"You know, there's an old saying hereabouts, Charlie. Nothin's certain but death, taxes, and Texas. Well, you're starin' a quick trip to sulfurous perdition right in the face. Just as sure as range-crazed longhorns, given any chance at all, will hook a man in the liver. Suit me right down to the floor if you went on ahead, made a grab for your pistol. You'd save Uncle Sam's overburdened taxpayers the cost of housin' your sorry ass till he can hang you for those two brutal murders."

Bugg's lips peeled back over tobacco-stained, sharp, canine-shaped teeth. "Don't believe a word you say, mister. Known a company of deputy marshals in my time. Ain't any other federal lawdog ever talked to me like you just went and done. Never run across one of 'em yet as had balls any bigger'n a bumblebee's and grit enough to go an' threaten my life."

Longarm's grin got wider. "You're not confronted with just any federal lawdog, Charlie. I'm the one that will happily put four two-hundred-and-fifty-five-grain slugs in your guts before you can spit. No farther than we are apart right now, might even be able to lodge all six of 'em in your sorry hide. 'Sides, I'm bettin' a coward like you can't work up enough moisture to spit right now anyhow."

A stricken look of dawning terror flashed across Bugg's liquor-flushed face.

"Now," Longarm continued, "careful as a barefoot tarantula walking through a bed of hot coals, want you to reach across your belly with your left hand, unbuckle that belt, and let your pistol drop. Then lift the whole rig up and place it on the bar. My friend, Mr. Troop, will ease over and take charge of it for me."

Fingers of Bugg's right hand twitched and trembled.

Almost imperceptibly, Longarm shook his head. "You so much as blink the wrong way doin' what I just instructed, and you'll be shakin' hands with horned Satan the very next instant. 'Bout a second after that, figure he'll be jabbin' you in your stupid, murderin' ass with a red-hot pitchfork."

Of a sudden, all movement inside Buckhorn's Lame Dog Saloon appeared to cease. Paralyzing tension in the room shot all the way to Spider Troop's fancy, embossed, painted tin ceiling. The collective, momentary pause in shuffling, talking, drinking, and breathing, by almost all of Troop's afternoon tipplers, brought the unexpected, muted sounds of creaking floor timbers, whirring celing fans, and the ticking of a banjo clock on the wall to the forefront of Longarm's strained hearing. Sweltering cantina suddenly became quieter than the bottom of a fresh-dug grave at midnight.

It was as though bony, skeletal-faced Death himself had boldly ambled through the batwings, then leisurely taken a spot amongst the other booze hounds. Propped his razor-sharp, soul-reaping scythe against the bar. Beckoned to Spider Troop with fleshless fingers and ordered a tall, frosty-cold glass of beer.

Longarm's darting, concentrated gaze swept over Charlie Bugg from hat crown to silver-mounted Mexican spurs at least three times. He continued to tap the grip of his Colt with one clicking fingernail. "Don't have all day, Charlie," he growled. "Make up your feeble-assed mind. Unbuckle your pistol, or get that smoke-pole out and get to work."

One corner of Bugg's cruelly misshapen lips continued to twitch. Beads of salty sweat popped from beneath his hatband and ran down both sides of his scarred face in fast-moving streams. Then, to Longarm's surprise, the murdering bandit said, "'S one helluva tale you're tellin', mister. But just what makes you think anyone here believes you're actually what you've declared? Ain't seen no badge as yet. You got proof as to what you're claimin'? Far as I can tell, you could be just any lyin' skunk come in here to raise a stink. Try and make a name for yourself by offin' a big doer like me."

Between gritted teeth, Longarm snarled, "Gotta lot a damned nerve, you stupid wretch. If you think I'm gonna drag my wallet out to retrieve my badge, or haul out my bona fides while you go for your pistol and gun me down, you're 'bout a bubble and a half off plumb. 'Sides, rubbin' out a *big behaver* like you won't take much effort. Now, get to unstrappin' that pistol, you son of a bitch. Your time on this earth's fast runnin' out."

Bugg appeared on the verge of a total body twitch. His piggish eyes flared open, then began to rapidly blink like paper window shades accidentally released and flapping on a busted roller. Longarm figured that most of those bearing witness to the confrontation would have readily bet everything they had that the outlaw was on the verge of whipping his weapon out and blasting the tall stranger straight into the following week.

To the whole room's shared surprise, and relief, Bugg suddenly groaned as though all the spirit had drained from his quivering body. His whole body appeared to sag inward. Then he snatched at the shiny buckle of his pistol belt and threw the rig onto the saloon's fancy marble bar. Both hands fluttered toward the ceiling when he said, "There, there. It's done, mister. Unarmed. You satisfied. Even got my hands up. Ain't no need to do any shootin'."

"Got any hideout guns on you, Charlie?" Longarm growled.

Bugg grimaced as though someone had dropped an anvil on one of his feet. Under his breath, he muttered, "Damn." Then he said, "Okay. Okay. Hold your water. Now be careful, Marshal. Wouldn't want you to make a mistake and accidentally kill the bejabberous hell outta me." With one hand kept as high as he could reach, he stooped over and fished around inside the top of a stovepipe boot, then pitched a short-barreled .38-caliber Merwin and Hulbert revolver onto the bar alongside his belt gun.

The weapon hit the bar's lovingly cared for top, and bounced before Spider Troop could grab it. "Damn. Be careful, you stupid son of a bitch," Troop yelped. "This here's genuine Italian marble. Don't have a scratch on it. Won't have an ignorant cocksucker like you damagin' it."

Bugg whirled around as though he intended to climb over Troop's pride and joy, then stomp a bloody ditch in the drink slinger's haughty behind. "Best shut the hell up, Troop. Got no use for saucy-mouthed bartenders," he roared. "I ever get back out this way again, gonna remember what you just said. Wouldna had the spine for such nervy behavior till this badge-totin' son of a bitch showed up."

"That all of it, Charlie?" Longarm called out.

Bugg flicked a guilty look over his shoulder. "Yeah, that's it."

"Absolutely sure you don't have any more weapons on you? Wouldn't wanna discover you'd lied to me. Might just have to kick your ass till your nose bleeds, then stomp on you till you cough up whatever else you're hiding."

Bugg whirled around, jerked his vest to one side, then slid a bone-handled, ten-inch bowie from a leather scabbard jammed inside his pants. He flipped the knife into the air and grabbed the blade, then grinned and handed the glistening piece of steel grip-first to Spider Troop.

"You're certain there's nothing else?" Longarm asked.

"That's all of it. Swear 'fore Jesus. Ain't got nothin' else on me."

Longarm slipped his pistol from its holster. He flipped the muzzle at Bugg, then said, "Step outside, Charlie. Head on down to Buckhorn's lockup. Sure you already know where it is."

Bugg shuffled to the boardwalk like a tired bear forced to do three shows a day in a traveling circus. Without waiting, he turned toward Buckhorn's jail. Over one shoulder, he said, "Bet the damned jail in this burg is a real snake pit."

Chapter 5

Three days after suffering through the most humiliating half hour of his entire outlaw life, a dejected and humiliated Charlie Bugg used shackled hands to rein his tired horse to a halt beside and slightly behind Longarm's mount. The pair sat their animals on a sandy hill outside the leafy green hamlet of Val Verde. The prosperous-looking village spread out before them along either side of a striking central thoroughfare at the junction of the Pecos and Independence Rivers—almost exactly halfway between Fort Stockton and Buckhorn. The settlement's lush, tree-lined main thoroughfare and well-kept, freshly painted buildings appeared grossly out of place, given the endless stretches of rugged, barren, snake-infested, desertlike terrain that surrounded it.

As though lifting anvils, Longarm pulled a pair of nickel cheroots from his sweat-drenched vest pocket. Aching and feverish, he stoked both cigars to smoking life with a lucifer scratched across the butt of his Colt Lightning. He handed one of the tightly rolled sticks of tobacco to his disconsolate, manacled captive.

Bugg nodded grudging appreciation, took the cigar, and immediately sucked down a lungful of the heavy, rum-soaked, satisfying smoke. He blew a bluish gray ring the size of a wagon wheel heavenward. "Damn, that's mighty good," he mumbled, then took another healthy drag.

"Know you're gonna have to tell me sooner or later. We've got plenty of time," Longarm said.

Bugg picked a sprig of tobacco off his lip, then said, "You been at me ever since we left Buckhorn. Ain't tellin' you nothin' 'bout what got done with the money. Might as well give it up, lawdog. Forget about it. Wastin' your time and mine. 'Sides, if'n I did break down and tell, my partners would hunt me to the edges of perdition and back, then kill me deader'n a rotten fence post. Sure as crickets cain't pull Baldwin steam engines."

Longarm wiped the sweat from his fevered, dripping forehead with an already damp bandanna. Used the rag to swab out the inside of his saturated hat. Stuffed the flat-brimmed Stetson back on a broiling head, then swiped at his dribbling, snotty nose with the clammy piece of cloth. He hocked up a gob of phlegm, spit, then stuffed the bandanna back into his pocket.

"Them four bags of ill-gotten loot I found in your room ain't gonna satisfy any of my superiors, Charlie. Didn't amount to much more'n twenty thousand dollars all told. You don't give up the rest, or whatever you can supply of the rest, you're in a pit fulla shit."

Bugg blew smoke into a cloudless sky, then let out a cackling spurt of laughter. "Hell," he said, "I'm already in a pit fulla shit. Gonna hang anyway fer them two fellers what got kilt. Didn't shoot either of 'em myself, but if you're lucky enough to get me back to Denver alive, I'll swing for certain sure."

Longarm twisted in his saddle, rubbed a sore, aching back, and grimaced. "Well, can't argue with reasoning like that," he said. "But in my opinion, it'd be a helluva stupid act to take the location of all that money to the grave."

"Pretty sure my partners wouldn't come anywhere's close to agreein' with you about that'un, Marshal."

A chest-rattling fit of coughing doubled Longarm over

his saddle horn. He snatched his bandanna out, held it over his mouth, then wiped at his runny nose again. "Shit," he said, then spit a gob of greenish glop the size of a guinea hen's egg.

A wicked, fleeting grin flickered across Bugg's chapped lips. "Looks and sounds like at 'ere cold a yern is gettin' worse by the minute, Marshal," he said.

The murderous thief's captor reached over one shoulder and massaged a sweat-saturated spot that throbbed like he'd been hit across the back with a long-handled shovel. "Yeah, got this nasty rumblin' sensation in my chest. Head feels like a bagful of gelatinous beef fat. Eyes been itchin' somethin' awful ever since we left Buckhorn." He ran a shaky arm across a drenched face. "Sweatin' like the proverbial barnyard pig, too."

Bugg suppressed another self-satisfied smirk that could have easily turned into a mocking laugh had his situation been even the least bit different. The brigand's delight at Longarm's discomfort almost bled through when he tried to sound sympathetic by saying, "Damnation. Why, that's just terrible, Marshal Long. Be willin' to bet the ranch you're comin' down with a gut-wrenchin' case of the ague. Think might near everbody in Buckhorn had the shit when I got there month or so ago. Whole fuckin' town 'uz croopin', blowin' their noses, and a slingin' all kinda bodily fluids here and yonder. One feller died of it. Can't begin to imagine how I missed comin' down with a dose a the wretched stuff myself. Must be angels lookin' out for me. Some kinda God-sent miracle, I suppose."

Longarm sniffed, then stared off along Val Verde's main thoroughfare. "Oh, yeah, Charlie, I'm sure that's got to be it. Bein' as how you're on such good terms with the Diety. Sure he spends most of his days worrin' 'bout your health and welfare—sendin' out heavenly guardians just to protect your sorry ass."

Bugg feigned offense. "Well, yeah, could be. Hell, my momma taught me as how God loves all his creatures. Even the baddest kinda men, like me."

Bleary-eyed and sporting a nose swollen to the size of a sweet potato, Longarm motioned the outlaw ahead. "Creature's a good word to describe you, Charlie. Now, get on out in front of me a bit," he said. "Didn't want to stop in Val Verde for any length of time, but looks like I'm gonna have to put myself in the care of a sawbones. If these folks have a decent one."

Bugg grinned and guided his animal around Longarm's mount, Sneezer. "'S okay by me. Hell, be nice to find a bit of shade and get outta this skull-bakin' sun for a bit."

"Had wanted to get on to Fort Stockton. Hop the narrow-gauge to El Paso, then the train to Denver. Hadn't been drag assin' around 'cause of this 'bout of fever and chills, figure we woulda been there sometime early tomorrow. Way I feel right now, though, reckon it'll just have to wait."

Longarm and his prisoner waded their hay burners across the slow-moving, brackish, ankle-deep Independence River, then urged the tired, plodding beasts past a hand-carved welcome-to-our-town sign the size of a doubled-up barn door. Barely fifty feet past the imposing billboard, they ambled onto the broad, immaculately maintained expanse of Val Verde's main thoroughfare.

Drifting clouds of dust that had billowed and swirled around their animals' feet played out, then wafted away as they rode onto a fancy limestone-paved street, shaded here and there with cottonwood and live oak trees. Longarm caught himself thinking the boulevard was vaguely reminiscent of the kind of plant-lined avenues a body might see in Austin or Dallas. He'd passed through Val Verde a week before, but the urgency of running Charlie Bugg to ground had prevented him from giving much in the way of attention to the settlement's pleasant, well-kept appearance.

As the shod feet of their broncs clicked and clacked on the street's fancy, hardened surface, Bugg pointed out a man with a shovel and broom, then said, "How you like that, Long? Even got a feller picking up horse fritters. Ain't that the damnedest thang you ever done seen?"

Longarm cast a drained, bleary-eyed glance at Val Verde's street sweeper, then scanned along either side of the thoroughfare, taking in all the visible parts of the board-walk. To his creeping discomfort, citizens on both sides of the street stopped on the wooden walkways, stared, pointed, and spoke to one another behind cupped hands.

Some folks stepped inside the stores, saloons, and cafés, then motioned for others to join them. Cherry-cheeked kids held their parents' hands and pointed. Apron-wearing shop-keepers stood outside their establishments and gawked, as though a pair of multiheaded carnival freaks had ridden into their town on the backs of mythical, never-before-seen animals brought from Africa's least explored regions.

One person stood out from the rest of the rapidly growing crowd that began to trail behind the sickly lawman and his captive. Tall, lean, gifted with that distinctly confident look of almost all West Texas women, she boldly strode to the front of the pack. Sand-colored hair, severely pulled away from her striking, angular, sun-bronzed face, was twisted into a single braid that fell all the way to a narrow waist.

For reasons he could only guess at, the fine-looking example of womanhood appeared more than just a bit interested in Longarm and his now-miserable-looking captive. She exchanged muffled, angry words and gestures with some of the other gawkers. Belligerently slapped at one leg with a leather quirt. And several times fiddled with the bone-gripped Colt Lightning pistol strapped high on her shapely hip, as though she teetered on the verge of pulling the weapon.

A sudden, undeniable sensation of uneasiness crept up Longarm's back and across his shoulders, then began to run up and down a chill-racked spine. He couldn't put an aching finger on the exact cause of his trepidation, but got the impression that something he didn't understand was definitely afoot. While the arm-waving crowd behind them grew louder by the second, then surged, receded, and surged again, he and Charlie Bugg continued on their slow amble toward the center of town.

Growing more uneasy by the second, the apprehensive lawman motioned for Bugg to hurry up, and pointed him in the direction of the fancy, hand-painted placard that boldly indicated the location of the local marshal's office. Along the way, they passed a dressmaker's, a saddle shop, a meat market, a sizable saloon named Crabb's Big River, a brick-fronted bank, hotel, gun shop, wagon yard, and mercantile. Val Verde's prosperity appeared undeniable.

Situated hard by a joint named the Big Canyon Café, the prosperous-looking settlement's substantial jail appeared a prime model for any growing municipality five times bigger than the pissant-sized burg. Imposing sets of hardened-steel bars covered all the hoosegow's observable windows. The front door was a single, massive slab of oak, reinforced with thick iron bands and matching hinges. Didn't take Custis Long but about a second to formulate the opinion that a box of dynamite and a pickax couldn't have taken the door down.

Longarm reined up at a hitch rack less than ten steps out front of the pokey's entrance. As though bent beneath a heavy burden, he hit the ground on both feet at the same time, then tiredly motioned Bugg off his animal. When he grasped his prisoner by the elbow, the worn-out deputy marshal noted that it felt as though most of the strength seemed to have drained from his aching body. He ushered his captive onto the boardwalk, pushed him across the jail's threshold, then carefully closed the impressive building's heavy entryway behind them.

As he had noticed on an earlier visit, the outer office of Val Verde's clink was the cleanest, neatest Longarm had ever seen. Place even smelled good. Most likely attributable to the polished wood floors and paneled walls. Not the slightest hint of the nauseating combinations of sweat, piss, puke, and rotting humanity characteristic of most rustic clinks assailed his nearly snot-plugged nostrils.

Handsome gent sat in a padded leather chair behind a banker's desk. He bore a striking resemblance to woodcut renderings of the heroic figures an avid reader would normally expect to find on the overheated covers of blood-and-thunder magazines. Kind of reading material that often depicted the gunfire-laced exploits of the handsome, stalwart, audacious lawmen of the untamed West.

A brilliantly white shirt, highlighted by blond hair and a pale, wheat-colored mustache, conspired to give the West Texas town's ruddy-faced badge toter a decidedly imposing, nigh on godlike appearance. A polished brass plate, attached to a block of triangular-shaped mahogany, sat at the front of the desk and had the name Hampton Forbes etched into it in flowing, flowery script.

Feeling ever so slightly uncomfortable in the presence of such a glorious being, Longarm placed his badge and packet of bona fides on the man's spotless writing surface. "Afternoon, Marshal Forbes. Hope you remember me. Name's Custis Long. Deputy U.S. marshal out of Denver. Came by a week or so ago. Just in case you don't recall my visit, though, should find all my letters of introduction, warrants, and such in order if you care to examine them."

Forbes leaned back in his seat. "Yeah. Seem to recall you stopping in. In something of a hurry, as I remember."

"Like to leave my prisoner in your jail for a night or two."

Forbes cast a less-than-interested glance at his dust-covered guests, then made an unenthusiastic effort at sifting through Longarm's pile of documents. He pushed back in his seat, pitched the warrant for Charlie Bugg's arrest onto the mound of papers, then eyeballed Longarm and said, "Yeah, remember when you stopped in, Marshal. Told me as how you were lookin' for this skunk, as I recall. Appears you found him."

Longarm flicked a bead of sweat from the end of his nose. "Caught up with 'im over in Buckhorn. We're on the way back to Fort Stockton. Need to put 'im up with you for at least one night. Maybe two."

Forbes arched an eyebrow. "You don't look at all well there, Marshal Long. You okay?"

"Can't say as I am. Have to admit, I'm not feeling very good at all. Be totally forthright, Marshal Forbes, that's why we're here. Normally, I wouldn't make such a request unless absolutely necessary. But given my present state of health, expect I'm gonna have to rest up for at least a few days 'fore headin' on over to Fort Stockton. Any problem with that?"

Val Verde's dapper lawman scratched his closely scraped, near-glowing chin with one finger. "Well, for me, none at all, Marshal Long. Not sure about a good many of the other folks here in town, though."

Longarm frowned, rubbed the back of his aching neck, then said, "What the hell's that mean?"

His question still hung in the air when the jail's heavy front door slammed open. Thick slab sounded like a pistol shot when it bounced off the section of wall between the door and front window. The long-legged, handsome woman Longarm had noticed in the street strode across the threshold with all the authoritative self-assurance of someone convinced she owned the place.

Forbes said, "Billie." The girl nodded, but appeared so angry she was having trouble speaking. Forbes made an offhanded motion in Longarm's direction, then said, "This here's Marshal Custis Long. Bringin' in a prisoner for me to take care of for a day or two. Say hello to Miss Billie Tyler, Marshal Long."

The glimmer of an interested smile etched its way across Longarm's tired face when he knifed a gander at the girl and noticed she had smoldering eyes a color of green he'd never seen before. It was a physical mystery located somewhere between jade, fresh growing grass, and chartreuse. Was impossible not to notice the fingers of darting, emerald-colored fire that appeared to flash at Charlie Bugg when Billie Tyler turned her blistering gaze in the still-shackled outlaw's direction.

Longarm tipped his hat and said, "Pleased to make your acquaintance, Miss Billie." The Tyler woman shot her fierce look in his direction, but didn't appear to see him.

Quivering like a leaf clinging to a dead limb in a windstorm, she whipped back around, pointed at Bugg with her quirt, then said, "You know he's the one that killed Buster, don't you, Hamp?" Then she snatched her pistol from its holster so fast, Longarm barely had enough time to jump in her direction and redirect the muzzle blast into Marshal Forbes's ceiling. The weapon's thunderous, booming report, confined by the smallness of the office, came nigh on to deafening everyone in the jailhouse's outer office, including the shooter.

Took about as much energy as Longarm could muster to wrench the still-smoking equalizer from the fiery-eyed gal's iron-fisted grip. He placed his free hand on the bare flesh, exposed by her open-throated man's denim shirt, and pushed her backward. Gal took a swing at him as she stumbled toward the wall opposite Forbes's desk, then clumsily dropped into one of a pair of cane-backed guest chairs. She started to hop back up, but thought better of the move when Longarm wagged a warning finger at her.

Red-faced, wild-eyed, and shocked right to the soles of

his boots, Hampton Forbes scrambled from beneath his desk. He brushed at dust on his clothing Longarm couldn't see, then shook his own finger at the trembling, emerald-eyed woman. "Dammit, Billie, I would've got around to discussing Buster's death with Marshal Long here if you'd a just given me enough time. Hell, I recognized this skunk soon as I saw him walk through the door."

Longarm's confused gaze swung from Forbes to the girl, then back again. "What in the blue-eyed hell are you two talkin' about? Didn't mention anything about Bugg killin' anyone named Buster during my last visit." He cut a darting glance in Charlie Bugg's direction. Bugg shrugged and tried his best to look as though nothing more surprising than a Sunday morning stroll to church services had just occurred.

Eyes still on the fuming girl, Forbes flipped his head in Bugg's direction, then said, "Six weeks or so ago, this man came through Val Verde. Had been in town about two weeks, causing various kinds of trouble, when he got into a drunken brawl with Miss Billie's younger brother, Buster, over in the Rio Grande Saloon. Buster ended up dead. By the time I could get across the street, your prisoner had vanished and left the boy lying atop a poker table with a six-inch Arkansas toothpick jammed through one eye."

Bugg turned both ironbound hands heavenward, shrugged, then said, "Ain't never been here afore in my entire life. Swear on my sainted mother's grave."

"That's a black-hearted lie," the Tyler woman snarled.

Then, of a sudden, Longarm caught the sound of a strange, atavistic groaning. It seemed to start somewhere deep inside the teeth-gritting Billie Tyler's guts. The growl rose through her chest and came out her mouth like the sound a body would expect to hear from a wounded panther.

To Longarm's stunned surprise, the screeching gal abruptly flew out of her chair. She went past the astonished lawdog in a blur of flailing arms, then jumped right in the middle of Charlie Bugg with both feet. Knocked the stunned brigand to the floor. Seated atop the yelping outlaw's chest, she proceeded to flay the flesh off his face with her everpresent riding crop.

Took damn near all of Longarm's rapidly dwindling strength to get a grip on the screeching female, then pull her off his wild-eyed, thrashing prisoner. He dragged the red-faced woman to the jail's front entryway, latched on to her collar, then pushed her toward the boardwalk.

To Longarm's shocked dismay, the thrashing female stumbled over the doorway's raised threshold, floundered, then fell in a crumpled heap and rolled into Val Verde's fancy stone-paved street. A group of nigh on thirty people who milled about in front of the jail witnessed the whole unfortunate affair. Several angry townsmen hustled forward and offered to help the red-faced gal to unsteady feet.

Longarm stood in the doorway, knifed a quick glance at Hamp Forbes, pointed toward the cell block, and said, "Lock Bugg up, Marshal. I'll take care of this mess out here in the street."

When he swung his attention back to the grumbling crowd, a lanky tough wearing shotgun chaps, a Texas-style Stetson, and a profoundly indignant look, had grabbed the scrambling Billie by one arm and was working to steady her efforts to stand.

The brush popper let the fingers of one hand linger on the Tyler woman's elbow. Then he shot a hard-eyed, frowning glare in Longarm's direction and said, "Got a habit of abusin' women, you ugly son of a bitch? Why don't you just get on out here in the street, and I'll kick your skinny ass till your nose bleeds. Box your ears till the wax pops out."

Dust flew in all directions as the Tyler woman whacked at her riding skirt and blouse. She glowered at Longarm and snapped, "That ugly bastard in there murdered my little brother, mister. And I intend to see he pays for his crime. Best get your mind made up to the fact. Get in the way and you just might not live much longer yourself."

Chapter 6

Mortified by the outcome of his clumsy attempts to separate Charlie Bugg and the irate Billie Tyler, Longarm stood on the boardwalk fronting Val Verde's jail. He removed his hat, then said, "Hope you'll accept my sincere apologies, ma'am. Didn't want or expect you to fall the way you did. Extremely sorry, but you've got to understand, I'm a deputy U.S. marshal, and the man you just assaulted is my prisoner. Cannot allow unarmed men in my custody to be shot or beaten before my very eyes no matter what kind of weasel they might be."

"Don't care if you're God Almighty," Billie Tyler snorted back. "Your *prisoner* murdered my brother. Your *prisoner's* a dead man and just doesn't know it yet. You try to stand between him and his inevitable fate, can't guarantee you'll see the next sunrise."

A rail-thin, skull-faced gent, dressed in a swallow-tailed black suit and silk top hat, patted the Tyler woman on the back and said, "There, there, Billie. I'm sure this gentleman didn't mean any harm. Bet he completely understands the situation now that you've so clearly explained it to him."

An angry cowboy at Tyler's other elbow growled, "No, he don't. None a them badge-wearin' bastards ever see things the way regular folks do. 'S some kinda blind spot they all develop when they pin on them tin stars. Hamp's only one I've ever met that's worth more'n a bucket a wet chicken shit."

Longarm held his hat low and tapped one leg with the brim. A wave of gut-wrenching nausea flooded over him. Along with his usually ironbound constitution, the stalwart lawman's patience with what appeared as a rapidly decaying set of circumstances had begun to wear thin.

In the full knowledge that he needed to disperse the crowd before some unthinking fool made the ultimate misstep and caused real problems, he gritted his teeth, then said, "Look, folks, can't have anything like the kind of behavior Miss Tyler just exhibited or has threatened. Now I think it best you all scatter. Go on about your business. Or go home."

When the already surly swarm of Val Verde citizens responded with a round of general grumbling and a raised fist here and there, he made an abbreviated shushing motion with both hands, then added, "Especially can't have such conduct goin' on inside, or immediately outside, the office of Marshal Forbes's jailhouse."

"'S our jailhouse. We paid fer it," someone in the churning crowd hollered.

Longarm ignored the comment. Acted as though he hadn't heard it. Waved his hat to try and gain a bit of quiet from the crowd, then said, "Good God, folks, the lady pulled a pistol and tried to shoot my prisoner."

"Too bad she missed," someone yelled to general laughter and hoots of blatant contempt.

"Look," the flustered lawman continued, growing angrier by the second, "I truly did not mean to hurt Miss Tyler. Sincerely hope all you good folks will see fit to excuse my somewhat ham-fisted efforts at bustin' up a fight on its way to becomin' a killin'." The crowd quieted a bit, so he added, "Now, far as I'm concerned, this discussion has gone on long enough. Time all of you were headed back to your own concerns and left the affairs surrounding Charlie Bugg in the capable hands of Marshal Forbes and me."

An unknown participant in the hubbub, who had secreted himself in the back-most ranks of the grumbling assemblage, yelled, "Murderin' skunk Charlie Bugg *is* our affair, you dumb bastard."

"Amen," shouted another anonymous member of the crowd. "Man you rode in with killed one of our most prominent and well-liked citizens, by God."

Marshal Forbes stepped up beside Longarm. Under his breath, he said, "Got your prisoner safely locked away, Marshal Long."

Longarm ran his arm across a sweat-drenched brow. "Well, thank God. At least somethin' has gone right today."

Then the thunder of horses' hooves pounding into town from the west drowned out several additional shouts of support for the irate Billie Tyler and further derision of the Denver lawdog. Took the passage of less than two seconds for Val Verde's horde of angry citizens to have their attention diverted toward the noisy approach of new arrivals.

Forbes made an offhanded gesture in the general direction of the coming riders, then said, "Case you're wondering, boys headed this way are Billie Tyler's three remaining brothers. Four of them own and operate the Twisted T spread ten miles or so out the west side of town. If you thought Billie was a handful, Marshal Long, just wait till this bunch of churnheads gets good and wound up. Especially the youngest one. Kid named Drew. Boy's a genuine ripsnorter if there ever was one. Short-fused and fiery as hell's own blazes."

From the corner of a misshapen mouth, Longarm hissed, "How come you didn't mention any of this hairball the last time I passed through your little slice of heaven, Forbes? Sure as hell mighta had second thoughts about stopping over again like I did."

Val Verde's marshal shrugged. "Well, Marshal Long, you were in something of a hurry, as I remember the occasion. Didn't seem to care a damn about anything that'd happened around these parts. Only wanted me to point you in the right direction, so you could find Charlie Bugg. Hell, I figured there was no point slowing you down with a detailed rendition of our little town's particular problems."

"Not much of an excuse, Forbes."

"Come now, Marshal Long. No need to be testy. Give the thing a bit more thought. Firmly believe you'll recall as how I did mention at the time that Bugg, during his brief stopover here in town, had in fact brutally rubbed out one of the locals. Seems as how you might've been on your way out my door at about that exact instant. In something of a rush at the time, as I recollect. But I did mention it."

Custis Long shook his head like an old dog with a flea in its ear. "Don't remember that. 'Course, the way I feel right now, you could spin the wildest windy whizzer imaginable of what occurred any more'n a week ago, Forbes, and I'm not sure a single minute's worth of living memory would still be with me that'd refute whatever yarn you might come up with."

As the Tyler brothers slowed, then urged their animals forward at a walk, the seething cluster of Val Verde's angry residents sucked back like a wave on a sandy beach. Billie Tyler pushed as many people aside as she could in order to let the trio of horsemen get up front of the fuming group. All the while, the angry woman continued to shake an accusatory finger at the two lawmen. And she kept up a venomous tirade concerning Charlie Bugg, her murdered brother, and her recent dance with the brute of a lawman standing in the jailhouse door next to their *supposed* friend Hamp Forbes.

A sudden hush and stillness fell over the throng as a wiry, hard-eyed gent, who bore a striking resemblance to his sister, stepped off a high-strung, palomino pony, then strode right up to the edge of the boardwalk. He came to a stop barely six feet from Longarm. Hooked his thumbs over a pistol belt studded with palm-sized, burnished-silver Mexican conchos. A well-oiled Colt pistol rode high on a narrow hip. He snatched a smoking cigarillo from between his lips, then cast an insolent glance at each lawman.

Hamp Forbes nodded. From behind a forced, tight grin, he said, "Good to see you, Drew."

Despite his muddle-headedness, Longarm recognized that Forbes's thinly disguised message was meant for him. Immediately, he redirected his fever-blunted attention from the mouthy, red-faced Billie Tyler and her peevish supporters to the man standing with his hand on the butt of his pistol a few feet away. The woman's brother appeared to have taken control of the volatile situation by simply showing his face.

The other two heavily armed riders dismounted and eased up on either side of Drew Tyler at about the time he snarled, "True what Billie's tellin' us, Hamp? You boys got that murderous bastard Charlie Bugg caged up in there?"

Forbes toed at a loose nail in the boardwalk, then studied the tip of his boot. "Can't deny it, Drew. Deputy U.S. Marshal Custis Long here rode in with Bugg in tow less than an hour ago. Got the snake that killed Buster locked up in back as we speak."

Tyler glanced from one of his squint-eyed, sneering brothers to the other, then said, "That a pure fact?"

"Yes. Yes, it is. And as soon as Circuit Judge Starns makes it back to town, we'll have a trial. Then we'll hang the son of a bitch."

As soon as word of a possible hanging fell from Marshal Hampton Forbes's lips, the crowd pushed the Tyler brothers' nervous mounts aside, and surged up behind the three new arrivals on the scene. It quickly became clear to Longarm that not a single soul in the noisy gathering intended to do a blessed thing until, and unless, the offended family decided on a particular course of action to follow. Leastways, that's what he secretly hoped.

Bigger, burlier man on the younger Tyler's right glared at Longarm and said, "Brother Drew's jus' tryin' to be a gentleman, boys. Ain't a person here today as gives a steamin' mound a steer shit 'bout no circuit judge. Don't care a tinker's damn 'bout no possible trial, or anythang like that. Got no way a knowin' the feelin's of the rest a these good folks behind us, but far as me, my brothers, and sister is concerned, you'd best march yourselves on back inside the jailhouse and get Charlie Bugg out here quick as you can. Or, if'n you'd prefer, we'll do it for you."

Longarm leaned toward Forbes, tugged on his hat brim, then hissed, "Who's this idiot?"

Forbes tilted his head in Longarm's direction and whispered back, "Oldest of the Tyler clan. Brother Wade. Wouldn't worry too much about him. More mouth than anything else. One who hasn't spoken yet is Jack. Might be the quietest, tamest-acting member of the whole damnable family, but he's also the most dangerous."

Longarm snatched his hat off and fanned a flame-red face. Muscles in his back and legs twitched; then it seemed as though every piece of sinew in his body coiled into a tight, ropy knot. Nauseous, head swimming, he came nigh on to doubling over at the waist.

Forbes placed a hand on his cohort's shoulder and said, "You okay, Marshal Long?"

With the expenditure of considerable effort, Longarm got himself erect again, then said, "Think so. Yeah. Yeah. I'm okay now."

In spite of the display of forced bravado, a hot, prickling sensation suddenly ran up and down the aching lawdog's spine and contradicted his optimistic assessment. He cast a watery-eyed glance over the jittery crowd again, and realized that his usually dependable powers of assessing such situations might well be on the verge of failing him.

The ugly awareness that the citizens of Val Verde were on the nasty, ragged edge of becoming a mob and taking the law into their own hands swept though Longarm's heaving mind like storm clouds from Mexico pouring over the Rio Grande. Worse still, short of a miracle, there didn't appear to exist a single thing in the world he or Hamp Forbes or the Good Lord Almighty Himself could do to stop them. Then, with those thoughts still thrashing about in his hectic brain, the entire dance flew all to pieces.

As though erupting from the depths of a sulfurous hell, the previously quietest of the Tyler family roared to life and yelled, "You men gonna let these cocksuckers keep Charlie Bugg locked up?"

Dozen or so members of the pack of townsmen gathered in the street yelled, "No. Hell, no."

Jack Tyler sounded like a traveling revivalist belching hellish flames when he waved his hat and screeched, "Bastard murdered my little brother, by God. Shoved a thin-bladed piece of steel into his eye. Hand of God had to have intervened to send this murderin' bastard back here to us like this."

The faithful appeared touched by the spirit of the moment. Someone produced a knotted rope. Others brought out their weapons.

Hamp Forbes held his hands out, palms down, then yelled, "Now, calm down, everybody. Can't let you go and do anything foolish."

Over the din of racket, an unidentifiable voice called out, "You ain't gonna give Bugg to us, then you'd best get the hell out of the way, Hamp. You boys don't wanna get hurt, move the fuck aside."

In a matter of seconds, Jack Tyler had managed to inflame friends and fellow residents to a level that sent chicken-fleshed shivers of dread up and down Longarm's sweat-drenched, ague-racked spine. Didn't take much in the way of rigorous thought to conclude that the entire front rank of Val Verde's citizens appeared to have an evil gleam in their eyes Longarm didn't like in the least. All three of the Tyler brothers and their fiery-mouthed sister were working like a quartet of cotton-chopping Alabama field hands to stir an already bubbling pot.

Of a sudden, Jack Tyler turned from the crowd and yelped, "Get 'em, goddammit. Get these badge-totin' sons a bitches outta the way." Split second later, the whole assembly had taken up the cry. A second after that, the noisy pack started moving.

Then, as if on cue, between thirty and fifty people strode forward as one. Arm-waving and bug-eyed, the crowd surged onto the boardwalk. The tidal wave of humanity filled the limited space in front of the jail like an empty water bucket in a typhoon. Press of shouting, fist-shaking humanity caught both lawmen with such decisive power and surprise, neither had time to get his weapon out or an arm raised in defense.

With stunning force, the enraged wall of Val Verde citizens hit Longarm. He staggered backward over the raised threshold and, just like Billie Tyler had a few minutes prior, stumbled. Then he went to ground like a sack of feed dropped off the tailgate of the local mercantile store's delivery wagon.

Laid low by the rapid turn of events, the scrambling lawman tried to roll onto one side. He doubled up and covered his face and head with both arms. Nothing he could do provided much protection from the assault. Booted feet hit him from every direction. By the time the gaping, purple-rimmed void of unconsciousness opened, and he had jumped into it feet first, Billy Vail's favorite deputy U.S. marshal felt reasonably certain every able-bodied man in

Val Verde had walked over, stepped on, stomped on, or otherwise kicked the living hell out of him. As he dropped into the more-than-welcome abyss of unknowing coma, words of thankful appreciation slipped from bleeding lips.

Chapter 7

Like a panicked swimmer, Custis Long struggled in his efforts at returning to a world of lucidity and light. He clawed at the walls of an all-enveloping, unending, leaden darkness, then relaxed a bit when cool dampness washed over his fevered, burning brow.

To the insensible lawman's amazement, people he hadn't seen in years, some of them long dead, stepped from the haze of dreamy unconsciousness and stood over him. They stared, clucked their tongues in seeming concern, and pointed. Some shook ghostly heads, or scratched their fleshless chins, as though in disbelief. Most spoke in languages he understood but didn't recognize.

Of a sudden, all those ghostly phantoms receded back into the swirling mists of sweating, pain-filled oblivion. Someone, speaking in a female voice he could not attach to a face, called his name. It took everything he could manage, but the redoubtable lawdog labored mightily until he was able to partially force one eye open. Then, after more arduous exertion, a tiny, cracklike gap finally let blurred light into the other eye.

Having spent what felt like an eternity in the murky gloom of semiwakefulness, Longarm blinked back painful tears at the brilliance of an unshaded window. He pawed at slitted eyelids with a numbly tingling hand that felt the size of a Colorado miner's coal shovel. The cool dampness returned. Momentary relief felt mighty good on a fevered forehead that ached and throbbed.

Then the same soothing, angelic, heavenly sounding voice returned and said, "You mustn't put your fingers anywhere near that eye, Marshal Long. It's badly swollen. So swollen, in fact, the lid itself has ripped open. Wouldn't want a wound so severe to get infected, now would we? Though the possibility is remote, you might never be able to see again."

Longarm squinted against the dazzling light source that appeared to come from somewhere not far from the bottoms of his feet. Took considerable concentration but, eventually, the hazy image of a woman standing near him loomed up from the sharp glare of recently returned awareness. He tried to sit up. His unthinking error in impetuous judgment was immediately evident. Every muscle in a battered body screamed out for mercy, as though a New Orleans stevedore had beaten him senseless with a knotted anchor rope. Then, just for good measure, the pain hammered him back into the bedclothes and mattress like a wooden tent peg being driven into soft ground.

"Aw, shit," he grunted amid the sweat-drenched bedding. "Shit a'mighty, that hurts. Hellfire and bloody damnation. Jesus H. Christ, have fuckin' mercy."

With great tenderness, a hand gently pressed against his shoulder. As though from on high, the blessed voice returned. "No reason to blaspheme, Marshal Long. None at all. I've never minded a bit of swearing. I'm well aware that men of your sort do tend toward a loose and vulgar mouth at times. Can't work for a doctor most of your life and not hear grown men swear in pain. But blaspheming is something I just cannot bring myself to tolerate."

He heard what sounded like water being squeezed into a porcelain washbasin; then the cool, moist compress hit his flaming forehead and throbbing eye again. "Thank you, ma'am. Appreciate the kindness," he said. "Hope you'll forgive my outburst. Not my usual behavior around respectable women, I assure you. But my God, been a number of years since I've taken a stompin' so thorough I can't even sit up. To tell the God's truth, ma'am, can't bring to mind the last time anybody gave me such a thrashing. Feels like all my nuts, bolts, and essential screws done got knocked loose."

"No need to apologize, Marshal. You've been through quite an ordeal. Assaulted by near fifty of my incensed fellow townspeople. Two and a half days in an addle-brained coma. A number of battered ribs. Fractured little finger on your left hand."

Longarm held the hand up. "Broke my finger? Sweet Virginia, broke my little finger."

"Doesn't begin to tell the tale, sir. You actually have contusions in places I didn't think a man could be bruised. And this eye. My word, if you've not been permanently blinded as a result of this particular wound, I'll be pleasantly surprised."

"Very much appreciate that piece of information, ma'am. Goes a long way toward explain' why I can't see for spit. But is the damage truly that bad?"

The woman tilted her head to one side and sucked air between pursed lips. "Appears as though someone brought a boot heel down directly into the socket. God-sent miracle such a blow didn't dislodge the eyeball itself."

Longarm groaned. He held the tingling, broke-fingered hand to his forehead again and squinted up at his handsome nurse, as though staring directly into the radiance of the sun. Took several seconds, but a gauzy, spectral image of blond hair, turquoise-colored eyes, and a damned fine figure finally congealed in his muddled brain. Near as he could tell, his caretaker was something of a beauty. Better a beauty than some horse-faced old crone, he thought.

"Truly?" he grunted.

"Indeed. That bad and more, sir. Wasn't for the fact that my father is, by far, the best medical practitioner within two hundred miles of where this all occurred, I feel fairly comfortable in saying you probably would not have survived the results of the worst thrashing I've ever seen perpetrated on a still-living person."

"Ah. Suppose there's some comfort to be taken from that."

"You're truly fortunate to have survived the first night of your time here in the recovery room of our office. Also helped that my father's practice is but a few steps west of, and across the street from, Marshal Forbes's office. He got you over here for the best treatment in West Texas within minutes of the assault."

A pained grimace etched its way across the injured, Denver-based lawman's scab-latticed face. Without warning, he jerked all over, as though in the throes of an uncontrollable seizure, or as if he'd suddenly remembered something important. "Two'n a half, almost three days? Did I hear you right earlier? Thought I heard you say I've been here nigh on three days, ma'am?"

"You heard correctly. In and out of consciousness the entire time, sir. Ranted and raved like a wild-eyed lunatic incarcerated in Travis County's iron-barred asylum most of that entire time. Often talked at great length with people who weren't in evidence—at least, not in this life. Couldn't make out much of what you were saying, but you did prattle on a bit. Seemed to spend a great deal of your time communicating with someone named Billy."

Longarm grunted as a tender but firm grip gently lifted an arm that felt as though it were being ripped from a socket filled with river-bottom sand. An agonized, involuntary groan escaped his dry, chapped lips. For the first time, the putrid, odiferous stench of dried blood and crusted bodily fluids, and the acrid taste of vomit, raked through barely functioning, stuffy nostrils. His swollen tongue felt like a dried, meaty slab the size of a hay bale with the coarse texture of a well-used saddle blanket.

He raised a bit of saliva, licked parched lips, then said, "Jesus, I must smell to high heaven, ma'am."

"True. Very true, sir. In addition to your physical injuries, you also suffered from an acute bout of ague when brought to us. Your fever broke last night. All the sweating typical of such a renewal has made quite a mess of you, I must admit. You need a good wash, sir. Along with an immediate change of sleepwear and some fresh bedding."

"Ain't that the truth."

"Yes, well, hated to disturb you, but that's why I'm here this morning. We're going to get you cleaned up—as much as possible at any rate. Promise I'll do my level best not to cause you any more pain and discomfort than necessary."

With great skill and tenderness, she ran the cool, moist, soothing cloth down the length of his bruised, aching arm and then back up again. "Once I've finished with your bath, and got you into something clean to wear, I'll get you sitting up and change the sheets on the bed."

In an effort to diffuse the wicked, stabbing pain of being moved about, Longarm grunted, "Marshal Forbes? He make it through this dance alive, ma'am?"

"Yes. While our good marshal did not completely escape injury, his wounds were not nearly so severe as yours. Not nearly. I'm told that he returned to his office yesterday, and is trying to put everything back in order again."

"And Charlie Bugg? Feller I brought in and locked up in Val Verde's jail."

Through the gauze of restricted vision, Longarm detected a tired shake of his nurse's pretty head. "Ah, well, now, that's an entirely different story altogether. Must admit I wasn't aware of that ill-fated man's name. Hate to be the one to break the news, but your Mr. Bugg was not so fortunate as either of you gentlemen of the law, to tell the unvarnished truth."

"Lynched him?"

"Indeed, sir. Forced from his cell by a pack of screaming hooligans. Dragged to a massive, twisted, live oak hanging tree out on the west edge of town. Hanged by the neck until dead, dead, dead, as I've been told. Sent to whatever Maker he prayed to for final, eternal judgment. Haven't visited the horrid scene personally, but those who have tell me the poor man's festering corpse has yet to be taken down."

Longarm closed both eyes, flinched with pain, and groaned. "Sweet Virginia. Ole Bugg's been swingin' from a length of hemp for nearly three days in this scorchin' weather? Poor broke-necked bastard must be pretty ripe by now. Bet he's done gone and swole up to the size of a bloated heifer."

A slight hesitation in his nurse's ministrations gave Longarm the distinct impression that she was more than a bit affected by his brutal assessment. "Yes," she finally said, so softly he almost missed it. "Given the recent heat, I would expect that poor man's brutally stretched corpse is in quite a sad state by now."

Took near an hour to get Longarm thoroughly cleansed and outfitted with crisp, starched, and ironed bedding, along with a fresh undershirt and drawers to sleep in. He lay atop clean sheets and gazed at the bustling, indistinct image beside his bed. Wondered some at the implications of the lingering attention the more-than-attentive nurse had spent on his most private parts during her efforts at his abbreviated bath. And, while it smarted something fierce, he could not keep a fleeting, self-satisfied smile off battered lips. Then, still grinning, he drifted in and out of a heavy-lidded nap.

An opening door brought the aching lawman out of his doze. Though still barely able to distinguish little more than shape and movement, he realized his stunning caretaker was about to take her leave of him.

"Miss," he called out. "Please forgive my sad display of grossly poor manners, but what is your name?"

Burdened with what appeared to be a huge pile of his dirtied linens and bedsheets, she stood in the doorway, framed by the light pouring in around her fine, female figure. "Hughes, Nettie Hughes," she said.

Something like mild exhaustion had crept into her voice, he thought. "And your father's name?"

"Doctor C. Benson Hughes, formerly of Boston."

"Ah. Well, if the good doctor has the time and could stop in and visit for a minute, I would like to extend my sincere thanks for his medical expertise and kind attention. Appears he's done a first-rate job of patchin' my stringy behind that was near stomped all to pieces."

A thoughtful pause preceded the handsome woman's reply. Then she said, "I am hopeful my father will return sometime before dark today, sir. However, there exists the very real possibility that such might not prove the case."

Longarm shifted in the bed and groaned. "How so?"

"A rider for the Big Canyon Ranch came in early yesterday morning. Seems one of their best hands, Jesse Coaltrane, was thrown from his animal. Poor man landed on his back across a corral railing. He was in a bad way."

"Jeez. Sorry to hear such a tale."

"Well, Marshal, given that the Big Canyon spread is forty miles south of town, it could be as late as tomorrow afternoon before my father makes it back to Val Verde. His return depends on how severely that poor cowboy was actually hurt."

"Sad tale. Truly sorry to hear such."

"It's nothing more than daily life in the West, as I'm sure you're well aware, Marshal Long. Men, women, and children die at an alarming rate out here in the wilds of Texas." She turned and started to pull the door closed, then stopped and said, "I'll be in the office until it gets dark should you need anything before then. Our home is but a few steps out the back entrance, directly behind this building. I'll check in on you at least once or twice during the night." With that, the door clicked shut and she was gone.

Within minutes of Nettie Hughes's departure, the god-awful-tasting laudanum took hold. The cruelly abused lawman slept like a hibernating Montana grizzly bear. An experienced Civil War gunner could have fired a Napoleon cannon at the foot of his bed and Deputy U.S. Marshal Custis Long would not have moved a single, aching, stringy muscle.

Chapter 8

The next time Longarm came fully awake, his vision seemed to have cleared somewhat—enough that he could distinguish faces at any rate. A bearded gentleman, who sported pince-nez glasses and a pin-striped, vested suit, was shoving the metallic bulb of a stethoscope around beneath the sheet draped over the injured lawman's chest. The doctor flashed a quick smile, nodded, then made studiously concerned sounds.

A few feet from the foot of Longarm's bed, Marshal Hamp Forbes leaned against the open window's frame and puffed on a Mexican cigarillo. In spite of Nurse Nettie Hughes's description, Longarm could detect no obvious wounds to Forbes' imposing person. Near as could be ascertained, Val Verde's lawman looked exactly the same as he had the day they'd first met. That particular piece of prickly knowledge stuck in Longarm's craw like a fist-sized cocklebur, and caused him to twist the sheet by his side into a tight knot.

Val Verde's badge toter held the pencil-thin, smoldering cigar between his fingers, rolled it back and forth, and said, "Reckon he'll live, Doc?"

C. Benson Hughes removed the listening device's metal ends from his ears. He folded the instrument's flexible tubing and slipped the apparatus into the worn, sagging pocket of his suit coat. Bending slightly at the waist, but making no attempt to probe the wound, the physician stared at Longarm's injured eye for several seconds.

"Oh, I think he'll mend, Hamp," the doctor said. "Must admit, though, I am a bit concerned about the prognosis for the damage to this eye. Probably looks worse than it really is. Still and all, it's an incredibly nasty and potentially dangerous wound. Somebody made a real mess of it."

Longarm pushed himself up onto one elbow. While still painful, the agony did not compare to his initial efforts the previous day. "Not gonna be blind, am I, Doc?" he said.

Hughes removed his dainty glasses, then tapped them against the thumb of his opposite hand. "Somewhat difficult to tell for certain, young man. This is only the fourth day since the initial injury. You're still badly swollen. Now that you're awake, I'll have Nettie bring ice from the Rio Grande Saloon next door. We'll try to keep the wound packed, as much as you can stand it anyway. Should bring the swelling down. Even so, might well take another ten days to two weeks, maybe even three, before we can get a good indication of just how much lasting harm the trauma caused. Once the eye's back to about half its present size, we'll cover it with a patch."

Longarm groaned, then eased back down into his mattress and placed one arm across his forehead. "Don't like the idea of looking like a Barbary pirate, but sure as hell wouldn't want to wind up unable to see any more than a roll of barbed wire, you know, Doc."

Hughes said, "While there are no definitive answers to all your questions at present, I do feel, young man, that right now it would be to your great benefit if we could get you up and moving around. Longer you're stretched out on your back, the better chance you'll have of coming down with a bout of pneumonia. Leastways, that's been my experience in the past. Wouldn't want that, now would we? Might not recover from such a malady."

"No. Suppose not," Longarm said. He strained back onto one elbow, then rolled onto his side and made a mighty effort at getting himself upright again.

Hughes moved to help his patient, but the injured lawman growled like a wounded grizzly, then brushed the doctor's hand aside. By the time Longarm finally got himself into a sitting position, thumb-sized beads of sweat decorated a flushed, furrowed, pinched brow.

"Damnation," the struggling deputy U.S. marshal said. Then he let out a lengthy, pained sigh. Four attempts later, he was able to stand on wobbly, trembling legs. "Not sure I can walk just yet, Doc. Mighty unsteady on my feet."

Hughes forced a tight grin. "Just do the best you can, Marshal Long—step or two now, step or two later. Trust me, simply getting up and down is most beneficial, but the more you can do the better."

With treacherous legs lodged against the mattress of the bed, Longarm swayed back and forth like a creek-side weeping willow in a stiff breeze. It would have appeared to any casual observer that he was locked in a furious attempt to build up energy and nerve. Then he abruptly stumbled across the room like a whiskey-weary brush popper on a two-day drunk to a low, dressing table.

He steadied himself by grabbing the oval-shaped mirror attached to the back of the piece of bedroom furniture. For a second, he could not recognize the reflection staring back at him from the grainy, silver-veined piece of glass.

Stunned by the image he saw, Longarm leaned closer to the horrific reflection. He ran shaky fingers along a bruised, stubble-covered, black-and-blue jawline. Then, as though fearful he might make a bad situation worse, he tilted his head a bit for a better view of the eye everyone seemed so concerned about.

The damage could not have been more apparent. The entire right side of his face, from a scruffy, scab-littered hairline to the tip of his handlebar mustache, appeared to be covered with a block of reddish brown, cracked, crusted blood the size of a grown man's hand. Looked almost as though someone had taken a blacksmith's horseshoe brush and tried to scrape off all the flesh. The eyelid was swollen to such an extent it had split apart. The ugly, jagged gash oozed a nasty-looking, greenish gray fluid from cracks in a second, softer and uglier, piece of caked, blackened, scabrous flesh.

Hamp Forbes blew a smoke ring out the open window, then said, "No doubt about it, local fellers who rushed my jail did quite a dance on you, Marshal Long. Have to admit I'm more than a little bit amazed you're still alive. A lesser man wouldn't have made it. Hope you'll accept my apology for not being able to keep them off of you when those blood-crazed boys ran riot the way they did."

"Opened the ball on us pretty quick, as I remember," Longarm said, then twisted his head to get a better look in the mirror at the less deleterious injuries to his face, neck, scalp, and upper chest.

Forbes nodded. "Only thing as kept me from being in about the same shape, I suppose, was that I managed to stay on my feet. Then, too, half a dozen of those law-breaking bastards grabbed hold of my arms and kept me pinned against the wall. Please believe me, sir, I would have helped you had there been the least possibility of accomplishing such a feat."

"Well, that goes miles toward explainin' why you don't appear to have suffered much in the way of life-threatening injury yourself."

"Yes, well, unfortunately, you went down like a gunnysack full of horseshoes. Screaming horde of idgets forced me to just stand there and watch what they did. And, Good

Lord Almighty, seemed as though every son of a bitch in the mob took a turn stomping the hell out of you. You've got to be one stringy-muscled, tough son of a bitch, Long. Doubt there's a son of a bitch in town who could stand toe-to-toe, man-to-man with you."

"Speakin' of horseshoes, and the hair-covered beasts they're attached to, where's my animal?"

"Bell's livery and stable operation. Right down the street. Other side of the Rio Grande Saloon."

A sudden rush of unbridled panic swept over the injured deputy U.S. marshal. "And my saddlebags, weapons, and such?"

"Locked in the safe in my office."

"Merciful God. You look inside 'em?"

"'Course I did. Considerable amount of money you're hauling around in those bags."

"Yeah. Sure as hell is. Thanks for takin' care of it for me. Appreciate it."

Longarm wobbled back to the bed. With agonizing slowness, he eased onto the edge of the mattress. Much-abused lawdog felt as though his entire body throbbed with every strained, thunderous beat of his heart. To his utter surprise and dismay, even the muscles of his narrow, stringy ass hurt.

"You arrest any of 'em sorry-assed sons a bitches what done this to me yet?"

A rueful snort escaped Forbes's lips. "Arrest? Who am I going to arrest? Nigh on every able-bodied man in Val Verde who claimed Buster Tyler as a good friend? No place to lock them all up. No doubt about it, we've got a damn fine jail here in Val Verde. But there's not enough room for every warm-bodied man in town. And even if I did arrest each and every single one of them, couldn't impanel a jury within a hundred miles of here who'd have balls enough to convict the first man."

An overwhelming desire to lie down and go straight to sleep for about a year swept over Longarm. But the doc's admonition about moving around as much as possible still rang in scab-covered ears, and he knew he needed to stay awake. Best get myself up and shuffle-butt around some more, the battered lawdog thought.

He swayed to unsteady feet and trundled over to the tiny room's open doorway. Shambled back to the bed like a thousand-year-old drunk. Then, silently, made the same lumbering trip twice again.

Doc Hughes, who'd moved to the room's only entrance by then to give his stumbling patient some uncluttered space, leaned against the jamb and continued to tap the pince-nez glasses against his thumb. He watched as though amazed. Occasionally, he nodded and appeared thoughtfully pleased with his charge's concentrated display of single-minded determination.

Finally, appearing content with Longarm's efforts, Hughes made a harrumphing noise, then clipped the flimsy goggles back onto the bridge of his nose. He threw a casual wave over one shoulder as he turned away. "Well, I've other patients to see, Marshal Long. Several house calls to make," he said. "Keep up the good work."

Longarm hobbled across the room, as if trailing the good doctor, then watched as Hughes disappeared down a narrow hallway. He turned to Forbes and said, "While I fully realize Charlie Bugg was about as evil a no-account scamp as could be found suckin' air, you can't just let a violent lynchin' go by the board, Hamp." Breathing hard, he waddled away from the bedroom door, then gingerly took a seat on the edge of the bed again.

Forbes held his smoke out the open window and thumped an inch-long piece of ash onto the sill. "And what do you expect me to do, Long? Felt like I'd already explained. Any effort on my part in that direction would likely prove completely useless. And worse, just might get me killed deader than a rotten fence post for my efforts."

Longarm eased onto the bed's lumpy mattress and stretched out. "Well, then, soon's I'm able to get up and around, we'll sure enough try 'n arrest that entire, rock-headed Tyler bunch. Hit 'em with a charge of inciting to riot. If my once-pretty-good memory is still intact, none of the other participants dared to make a move until that family of idiots showed up and led the way."

With a shake of the head and wave of his cigar, Forbes dismissed Longarm's suggestion as if swatting away a nuisance blowfly. "Won't have any more luck arresting the Tyler boys than we would trying to arrest the whole town."

"Why not?"

Forbes shook his head in disgust, thumped his cigar out the window, and headed for the door. He paused in the entryway, turned, and said, "You're not thinking straight, Long. Not paying attention. Can't possibly believe, not even for a fleeting second, anyone around here's going to be responsible for convicting a single member of the Tyler clan for *inciting to riot*, spitting on the boardwalk, or anything else for that matter. If you do, you've got another gold-plated think coming."

"Well, now, that's just total bullshit."

"No. No, it isn't. Juries here in Texas have always taken a damned dim view of known murderers like Charlie Bugg. And as a consequence, live-oak string-'em-ups and let-'em-swing justice in these parts isn't what anybody would venture to call *real uncommon*." With that, he shoved his hat back on and headed down the hallway Doc Hughes had recently used without saying another word.

Finally alone, Longarm squirmed further into his bedding in an excruciating search for something like a comfortable spot. The bone-deep, aching agony that racked his contusion-covered body continued until dusk crept into the room's open window and Nettie Hughes once again appeared by his side.

"Have a draught my father prepared for you, Marshal Long. If you can find the strength to sit up, it will be a lot easier for you to swallow."

He squinted up at the woman he could now see far better than the previous day. A quick, fleeting look swept over full, pouting lips, upturned breasts, a tiny waist, and flared, muscular hips. Much to his satisfaction and approval, Nettie Hughes was one helluva good-looking woman.

He flicked a confused, one-eyed glance at the foggy liquid in the glass she held. "What exactly is it?" he said.

"Just a few teaspoons of laudanum mixed with a bit of pretty good whiskey. Should do wonders for your aches and pains."

"Laudanum? 'S opium, ain't it?"

"Yes. Yes, it is. Come on now, sit up and take your medicine, Marshal Long. It'll help with your pain. During the time you were unconscious, I administered this same dosage three times daily. Appeared to be of great benefit. Will make you more comfortable and help you sleep. Come on now, take it."

Longarm battled onto his elbow again, took the glass, and gulped down a swallow of the rusty, amber-colored, wicked-smelling liquid. "Jesus, that's awful," he snorted. "Tastes like the doc mixed bad snuff in good whiskey. Bitter as sulferous hell."

Nettie lifted the glass back to his chapped, cracked lips with one finger. "Finish it off. You'll sleep better. Trust me."

Longarm threw the bitter, snuffy-tasting liquid down in a single, quick gulp. In no time at all, the promised relief of painless sleep fell on him like an oak tree dropped from heaven's front gate.

Dope-induced dreams that night were filled with Nurse Nettie Hughes's gasping, grasping, naked, sweat-covered body. So vivid were his fevered reveries that on several occasions he awoke to find himself plagued with a doniker that was as hard as the blued, steel barrel of a Sharps Big .50. He couldn't help but wonder if the girl had snuck back in and washed it again while he slept.

Chapter 9

With the dutiful, near-undivided attention of Nettie Hughes, and the constitution of a bull elk, Longarm's painful recovery progressed apace. Within the short span of a week, he'd grown strong enough to accompany his beautiful, dedicated caretaker on walking tours around town.

Only took one such outing for the limping lawman to realize that he recognized a number of the smiling, hat-tipping locals he and Nettie encountered on the boardwalks. He knew, beyond a shadow of doubt, that the grinning skunks were one of the dozens of *gentlemen* who'd stomped the living hell out of him when they raided the jail and dragged Charlie Bugg's pitiful ass to the hanging tree. And while that galling realization infuriated Longarm, he knew nothing much could be done about it—at least not at the time.

The handsome couple's strolls always started on the boardwalk outside Doc Hughes's office door, then leisurely progressed up one side, then down the other, of Val Verde's often busy, stone-paved main thoroughfare. The pill wrangler's beautiful daughter preferred to go east first, so she could spend a few minutes dawdling outside the frost-etched, beveled-glass display window of Dobson's Mercantile and Furniture Store. She explained that Hiram Dobson's clerks changed the elaborate exhibit daily in an effort to entice local female shoppers inside. A ruse designed to win away prospective shoppers from his most ardent competitor, Hubert Lawson, who owned a similar-sized dry goods operation almost directly across the street.

On their second or third excursion, Longarm turned his still-swollen, patch-covered gaze sidewise at the couple's reflections in Dobson's enormous sheet of plate glass. He cut a blinking, one-orbed glance at their handsome images and realized that he and the striking woman at his side could easily have been mistaken for any attractive married couple out for a Sunday morning, after-church stroll. The surprising insight came as such a shock that, for several minutes afterward, he found it difficult to offer coherent replies following Nettie's almost endless string of daily observations, made for the benefit and edification of her one-eyed charge.

Once they had ambled past Tarantula Jack's Gun Shop, the Bishop Hotel, Burk's Meat Market, and the Rusty Spur Liquor Emporium, the attractive couple crossed over to the north side of Main. They made a slow about-face and continued their constitutional while gazing into the windows of Wilson's Dress Shoppe, Lawson's Dry Goods, the Wagon Wheel Saloon, Peterson's Clocks, the Big Canyon Bank, and, of course, the Davis Brothers' Shoe Shoppe for Fine Ladies.

It was while viewing a particularly attractive pair of dove-gray pumps that Nettie Hughes squeezed Custis Long's arm and said, "You may not be aware, Marshal Long, but the restaurant in the Bishop Hotel has a fine luncheon plate. It would be my great pleasure if you would accompany me there today for a bite to eat."

Longarm's only working eye twinkled as he leaned closer and said, "Why, Miss Hughes, I do declare. That's mighty bold of you, isn't it? I mean, it's not often a lady of your obvious good upbringing and community stature asks out a rough ole cob like me."

The Hughes woman tugged at his arm again, as though trying to draw him even closer still. Under her breath, and for his ears only, she said, "Do not be misled by my carefully crafted outward appearances, Marshal Long. As you should have surmised by now, I am a widow lady. And one somewhat starved for attention at that."

"Well, to be frank, I'd not thought of you as such at all. Don't exactly cover yourself in the drab, black raiment of a widow. But I had surmised that perhaps—"

Before he could finish his thought, Nettie Hughes said, "Horace was murdered several years ago."

"Ah. I see."

"No. I doubt you do. His death shocked me to the core. We had celebrated our fifth anniversary only a few days before his demise. Mr. Fuller was a fine man and did not deserve his fate."

"Fuller? Horace Fuller, huh? I take it you did not choose to keep his name?"

A trembling chin fell to the ruffled neck of the pristine, white blouse beneath her stylish sky-blue dress. "No. I had more than enough grief to remind me of my loss, Marshal Long. Did not require a minute-by-minute reminder to pop up every time someone called me by Horace's family name."

Longarm decided it best to let the subject lie for a spell. He turned, his arm looped over hers, leading Nettie Hughes away from the shop's wish-filled display and, thence, back across the street to the Bishop Hotel.

Once seated at the restaurant's best window table, overlooking a goodly expanse of Val Verde's attractive central thoroughfare, he opened his leather-bound menu, leaned forward, and whispered, "Your suggestion was a good one—one that I had considered myself, as a matter of fact. So, let us please deem this as having been my idea. Shall we, Miss Hughes? Couldn't live with myself if you didn't let this be my treat."

"Nettie, Marshal Long. Please do call me, Nettie."

"All right, Nettie, but only if you'll humor me and explain how your husband managed to get himself foully murdered. Certainly, I'm well aware that raking through the tragedy won't be easy, but I must admit I'm more than a bit inquisitive, given the recent events in my life, of which you've been such a significant part. More important, I'm a very accomplished listener, and it seems to me as though the burden of Mr. Fuller's passing is one that I could help you with—if you'd allow me."

"Jack Tyler killed him." She closed the bill of fare, primly placed it beside her plate, then matter-of-factly added, "I'll have the chicken."

For some seconds after his tablemate's brutal and surprisingly frank pronouncement, Longarm slumped in his overstuffed, brocaded armchair. He stared over Nettie's shoulder at the passersby in the street, and could think of nothing to say.

After placing their order with a white-shirted, black-vested waiter who sported a waxed mustache and swath of glistening, pomaded hair, Longarm glanced from side to side to make sure no one could hear. Then he reached across the table, took her hand, and said, "Why on earth would Jack Tyler kill your husband?"

An almost undetectable flush rose in Nettie's cheeks when she said, "His reason is sitting at this table with you. In fact, you're looking into its eyes, and soul, at this very moment, Marshal Long." Then she leveled a crystalline, blue-eyed gaze on him that left not a single doubt that she believed every word of what she'd just said.

Longarm released the girl's warm, dry hand, then slumped back into his wondrously comfortable seat. He tapped the top of the table with a nervous, inquisitive finger. "Jack Tyler killed your husband? Did the deed because he wanted you?"

"Murdered my husband, Marshal Long. There is a very

distinct difference in the definition of those two words, as I'm sure a man of your profession is well aware. He murdered Horace as surely as we're sitting here waiting for our lunch to arrive."

"Tell me how it happened."

"There's nothing much to tell really. I've known Jack Tyler for a goodly portion of my adult life. He's spent most of that time sniffing around the hem of my skirt, as if I were a dog in heat. Spurned the hateful wretch in every way I could imagine over the years my father and I've lived in Val Verde. Thought, at long last, Jack had assumed his rightful place in the nether regions of my affections when Horace and I married. Little could I have imagined that what he was actually doing was waiting for the opportunity to take from me the one man in this godforsaken place that I dearly cared for."

Longarm suddenly wished he had left the subject alone. But he had stepped into Nettie's tragic loss with both eyes open and knew he couldn't back away. "How'd it happen?"

"Jack bullied Horace at every opportunity for years, until the inevitable occurred. Or so the story goes. The tale that everyone in Val Verde religiously subscribes to says that after one of Jack's particularly offensive overtures toward me, Horace rode all the way to the Tyler ranch and called Jack out."

"Are there witnesses to that singular event?"

"None that I'm aware of—other than members of the Tyler clan, that is. Folks around here are so afraid of that bunch, no one even bothered to question the veracity of the account they offered when they brought Horace's bullet-riddled body in and turned it over to Hamp Forbes."

Longarm breathed a silent prayer of thanks when the food arrived. For the next half hour, he picked at his slab of well-charred beefsteak. Nettie barely looked up as she inhaled a plate of Southern-fried chicken, mashed potatoes, and garden-raised green beans. Given the tragic circumstances she had just described, it amazed the somewhat stunned lawdog that she still had such a healthy appetite.

As he brought the final, forked chunk of the beefsteak toward his open, waiting mouth, he flicked a glance into the street, then said, "Uh-oh."

Nettie glanced up and saw Longarm drop his fork and fumble at a barren waist for the pistol he'd left hanging from a wooden peg near the door of his room in her father's infirmary. She caught the direction of his glaring, one-eyed gaze, and twisted in her fancy, brocaded chair.

"Who are they?" she said, and watched as a trio of heavily armed riders passed in the street not more than twenty feet from where she and Custis Long sat.

"One on this end, closest of 'em, ugly bastard with a face like a twenty-year-old Union Pacific Railroad map, that's Jennings Bugg."

"May God help us, he looks like the spawn of Satan himself."

"Son of a bitch's Charlie Bugg's younger brother. Guess there's more'n a good chance the devil could've sired the pair of 'em."

"And the girl in the middle?"

"Not sure about her. Could be a sister, I suppose. Been more'n a bit of back-alley reports as how Jennings and Charlie had one. Nobody ever mentioned that the phantom lady was such a looker, though."

Nettie sounded on the verge of panic when she pointed a reluctant finger and said, "Oh, my sweet heavens, Custis. Looks like they're heading directly for Hamp's office."

Longarm stood, dabbed at dry lips with a spotless napkin, then dropped it onto the table. His gaze continued to follow the passing band comprised of Charlie Bugg's family and a probable confederate.

"Think the feller on the other end, one all decked out in silver and black an' wearin' the crisscrossed butts-first, gun rigs, is Fast Eddie Bloodsworth. Vicious skunk's rumored to be a first-class man killer. Some folks claim as how he's sent as many as fifty unfortunate souls to meet their Maker. If so, Val Verde, and especially its marshal, is in for one helluva ride."

After hastily dropping a fistful of coins on the table for their meal, Longarm grabbed Nettie Hughes by the elbow and swept out of the Bishop Hotel like a quick-moving, summer thundercloud. Her full-breasted chest heaved and breathing came in short bursts as, back in the doctor's infirmary, she watched him yank the pistol belt off the wall peg and set to strapping it around his narrow, athletic waist.

She leaned against the door frame and said, "You're not up to this, and you know it. Still can't see out of that eye. Wouldn't do to remove Father's patch as yet. You're going into a bad situation with only half your vision. Don't you realize you're at a disadvantage here?"

Longarm snatched the Colt Lightening .44 from its oiled holster, flipped the loading gate to one side, and checked each individual shell. Shoved the gun back into the holster. As he tried to push past Nettie, she grabbed him by the arm, pinned him against the door frame, and pressed her lush body against his.

A trembling hand came up to his face and gently forced him into a passionate, tongue-sucking kiss that lasted for some seconds—during which time she brought her hips up and provocatively rubbed herself against him.

When their lips finally parted, she backed away and hissed, "Do be careful, dear Custis. It appears you'll be dealing with dangerous people. Most certainly wouldn't want the same thing to happen to you that happened to poor Horace. Not sure I could stand that kind of pain again anytime soon."

A confident smile spread across his lips. "Don't you go worryin' yourself, Nettie darlin'. I'm a professional. Deal with their type of slick-bellied snake all the time."

Shaky fingers came up to the eye patch. "You're at

something of a disadvantage at the moment, dear man. Not sure you realize what a handicap you must overcome just to stay even, given the condition of this eye."

He made a move as though to strip away the leather cover and gauze pad beneath. Nettie grabbed his wrist. She pushed the offending fingers aside, then covered the patched eye with her own hand, but didn't touch it.

"You mustn't do that," she said. "It's still much too early yet. Maybe a few days from now, but not today."

"All right, darlin'. As you say. I'll leave it on a few days more."

Nettie's hand dropped from Longarm's damaged eye, then came up between his legs. Expert fingers quickly found what they sought. She caressed him, then ever so gently squeezed.

"Why, Miss Hughes. My, oh, my," a surprised, grinning Longarm said. "'Pears as there's something of the bold-as-brass hussy bubblin' around behind that good-girl façade of yours."

Nettie's caressing became more insistent. She pressed her upper body against his and rubbed ample bosoms across his muscular chest. "Not all hussies work in the bawdy houses of Hell's Half Acre in Fort Worth and service passing cowboys for their hard-earned money, my dear Custis. Surely, a man of the world such as yourself has realized by now that the most talented and plentiful hussies are very likely married, settled, and have a houseful of cherry-cheeked children. Those selfsame women primly sit in church pews on Sunday, and enjoy the love and affection of their blissfully ignorant husbands and many friends and neighbors."

Longarm brought his hands up to her tapered waist, then slid them around to muscular buttocks that clenched and unclenched as they worked to rub her sex against his. Powerful fingers dug into Nettie's taut flesh and hefted her wondrously shaped caboose, as he pulled her against the stiffening saber of love behind the straining material of his skintight pants.

"Sure would love to see this dance carried to its logical conclusion," he whispered into her ear. "But right now, I've gotta go, darlin'. Feel your friend Marshal Forbes might be in sore need of immediate assistance."

Nettie Hughes, her eyes heavy-lidded, sounded drugged when she rubbed him with renewed vigor and said, "Go, then. But do be careful. I'll be waiting when you're done."

"Don't you worry 'bout me, darlin'," he whispered. "Take more'n a trio like the yahoos I just saw ridin' into town to keep an ole lawdog like me from coming back here to you."

Then Longarm placed his cheek against Nettie's. Let his hot breath caress her ear, then tenderly kissed the very edge of the shell-like appendage. When her body trembled against his, he broke away from the clinging woman, turned, and strode for the boardwalk.

As he flung the entry open, the flush-faced Nettie Hughes called out, "I'll check with Papa about the eye patch, Custis. Perhaps he'll recommend removing it. He's the expert, you know."

"Not a bad idea, darlin'. Don't want to jeopardize my vision, that's for sure. But given the folks we just saw ride into town, could very well be in need of both my eyes right soon."

A fleeting expression of pain flickered across Nettie Hughes's face. "Don't you dare go and get yourself killed, Custis Long. And whatever else you do, make sure Jack Tyler's nowhere to be seen. Watch your back. You get yourself back here to me. I'll expect you to be done with this in no more than an hour."

"Well, I'll sure 'nuff do my very best. You can bank on it."

Nettie's hot-eyed gaze lingered on Longarm's crotch for several seconds. She fanned pink-tinted cheeks with a fluttering hand and said, "God as my witness, Custis Long, if you're not back in an hour, I'll load Papa's shotgun and come looking for you."

With a tense grin and curt nod of the head, Long stepped across the office's threshold and pulled the entry closed behind him. For several seconds, he stood on the boardwalk and carefully fingered the hand-cut, black-leather covering Nettie's father had placed over his seriously mangled eye. Fortunately, there was no one else nearby to see the concern on his troubled face.

"Just give yourself some time," he said under his breath. "Ain't the greatest idea to go bullin' your way across a public street and into Hamp Forbes' office half blind and sportin' a ragin' woody in your pants. Might as well take a minute to calm down. Woman's really got you worked up. Gotta be thinkin' straight when you get across the street."

Longarm took several slow, deep, relaxing breaths. Grabbed his pistol belt, lifted and resettled the weapon at his waist. Flipped the hammer thong aside to ensure easy access. Checked everything one more time just to make certain the ivory-gripped, double-action handgun lay unencumbered in the cross-draw holster sitting comfortably against his left hip.

The deputy U.S. marshal took his time as he sauntered past the alleyway between Doctor Hughes's office and the Rio Grande Saloon. He stopped next to a porch pillar in front of the cow-country liquor locker, darting one-eyed, concerned glances on the saloon's heavy glass window and swinging batwing doors. Nothing seemed amiss.

He leaned against a whitewashed oak porch prop and fished a rum-soaked, nickel cheroot from his vest pocket. Scratched a match to life on the butt strap of his heavy, double-action .44, then put dancing, sulfur-laced flame to the finger-sized stogie. Flipped the still-smoldering lucifer into the dusty street. Then, as he brought his hand back, surreptitiously grazed his recently rampant love muscle—

just to make sure it wasn't still as hard as the head on a ball-peen hammer. Shook his right leg, then stamped his foot.

A quick glance across the street revealed that the animals belonging to Jennings Bugg, the fine-looking, mysterious woman, and Fast Eddy Bloodsworth were now riderless. They were tied to the hitch rack a few steps from Hamp Forbes's office door. Appeared as though all three of the grim-visaged riders had disappeared inside.

Teeth tightly clamped onto his smoke, under his breath Longarm said aloud, "Well, Custis, guess you'd best go ahead and get your stringy ass on over there. Get this dance started. Gonna be interesting to see what transpires, don't you think? Yep. Uh-huh. Should be extremely interesting, if nothing else."

With that, Longarm took a single deep drag off his smoke, stepped off the boardwalk, and ambled toward the Val Verde marshal's office. Stern-faced, he looked every inch like a man on a serious mission. Perhaps a bloody and death-dealing mission.

Chapter 10

Halfway across Val Verde's main thoroughfare, Longarm could hear the rambunctious commotion going on in Marshal Hamp Forbes's office. Sounded as though several different people were shouting at the same time. Couldn't tell exactly what was being said. Noticed that the racket had pedestrians nervously moving off the boardwalk and into the street. Appeared as though anyone who got near the jail's front door decided they had best get away from a noisy disagreement that could well turn into violent action. Longarm stomped onto the boardwalk, bulled his way inside, then slammed the jail's heavy door behind him with an authoritative thud.

Jennings Bugg, leaning over the red-faced city marshal's desk and shaking his finger, abruptly stopped yelling and came to full height. After a quick glance in Longarm's direction, his face lit up with the flash of surprised recognition. Ropy veins still bulged from his thick neck as he tapped the top of Hamp Forbes's desk with the finger most recently used in an attempt to intimidate Val Verde's marshal.

A twisted, repellent grin bled onto Bugg's chapped, cracked lips. He knifed a squint-eyed, fleeting look at the girl. Good-looking woman sat slumped down in one of the city marshal's guest chairs like a two-bit hooker in a Dodge

City whorehouse waiting for a cowboy to pick her out for a ride.

With one hand, the attention-grabbing, black-haired, blue-eyed beauty smacked a braided, silver-handled quirt against the stacked-leather heel of her knee-high riding boot. Clicked a nervous fingernail against the textured, rubber grip of the cross-draw Peacemaker Colt lying against her taut, table-flat belly with the other. Her smoldering, icy-pale gaze swept Longarm from toe to crown, then, ever so briefly, hesitated on his still-bulging crotch. A twitching grin curled the edges of full, pouty lips. Lips that had no earthly need of enhancement with a coating of painted-on rouge.

Fast Eddie Bloodsworth skulked in a corner on the farthest side of the crowded office. Near the barred cell block entrance in the back wall, the deadly gunny was decked out in nigh on totally black garb. His outfit was highlighted with a hammered silver hatband, elaborate matching belt decorations, and twinkling, silver-plated pistols. Worn butts-first, the weapons were ensconced in holsters mounted on a pair of belts draped across the man's narrow middle.

Longarm couldn't help but note that Bloodsworth bore a striking resemblance to a big-pincered Sonoran desert scorpion backed into the corner of some college-educated, bug collector's capture box. Brooding skunk picked at already clean fingernails with a ten-inch, buffalo-horn-handled bowie knife. Scowled when he and Longarm locked eyes, then spit a gob of gooey brown tobacco juice onto Hamp Forbes's near-spotless floor.

The glimmer of stunned recollection still played across Jennings Bugg's deeply scarred countenance when he tilted his head to one side like an inquisitive wolf and growled, "Well, I'll just kiss my very own big, nasty, hair-covered ass. If'n it ain't Deputy U.S. Marshal Custis By-God Long—widely known to all and sundry as the long arm of the federal fuckin' law, I'll eat a raw porcupine, quills and all, by God. No salt 'er pepper on the beast."

Longarm nodded and grinned. "In the flesh, Jennings."

Bugg raised an all-inclusive arm and thereby waved his companions into the conversation. "Yes indeed. Billy Vail's favor-ite. I'm tellin' you, friends and relatives, his number-one, favor-ite hench-man. This gun-totin' fucker here ain't a man you'd want doggin' your trail."

Fast Eddie put his knife away and turned his whole attention on the new arrival. The wild-eyed girl sat up in her chair as though suddenly aware of imminent danger.

Longarm's grin widened a bit. "Haven't changed much, have you, Jennings? Still just as foulmouthed and disagreeable as ever."

Bugg feigned a horrified look of abject distress, then said, "You ain't lookin' too good there yourself, Long—arm. 'Pears to me as how somebody done went and whipped the dog shit outta your stringy, badge-totin' ass. Yeah, I'd say you done went and got yourself one helluva'n ass whippin'."

"Bad things have been known to happen to good people, Jennings. As any man with your kind of black-hearted background should well know."

Sulfurous, smoking hell flickered in Bugg's crazed gaze, but he kept his head. "Well, by God, hope 'fore I leave town you can introduce me to the vicious cocksucker what danced on your arrogant ass like that. I'll sure enough buy that man a drink. Yessir. Biggest, coldest'n he can find in this pissant-sized village fulla desert-addled idiots."

Longarm leaned against the front entrance's door frame and flipped his jacket away from the butt of his ivory-gripped weapon. Then, just to keep everyone off their balance a bit, he gallantly tipped his hat to the girl. Said, "Couldn't help but notice there's a lady in the room, Jennings. Might wanna get a grip on that astonishingly filthy yammerin' pie hole of yours. Know such an effort could prove somewhat difficult for a certifiable jughead like you. Could cause your cankered thinker mechanism to seize up like a wagon wheel ridin' on an ungreased axle. But why don't you go on ahead and give it a heartfelt try?"

Bugg threw a mangy, sweat-drenched head back and cackled like one of the inmates in an insane asylum. Cut his loony hooting off as if someone had slit his throat with a straight razor, then zeroed in on Longarm again and snarled, "Lady? Hell's fuckin' bells, she ain't no fuckin' lady. 'At 'ere's my baby sister, Bathsheba, by God. Gal's got more grit'n any man I ever met. And a worse mouth than her'n you'll never hear comin' outta me, or any other man as I ever run acrost."

The girl grinned at Longarm like a hissing, fork-tongued snake, then said, "Why don't you go fuck yourself, Jennings. Then go outside and fuck the horse you rode in on. 'S all you'll ever get, you ugly son of a bitch—'less you pay double for it. 'Sides, figure as how you've been doin' that animal so long already, I think she likes it."

Jennings Bugg threw his head back, laughed like a double-jawed African hyena, then shook his head and rolled bloodshot eyes. "Jesus Christ on a wooden crutch, Bathsheba. Didn't have to go and prove what I said. Coulda just kept shut, you silly-assed bitch."

Bathsheba Bugg slapped the stovepipe top of her boot with the quirt. While still darting guarded, hungry looks at Longarm's crotch, she licked full lips and said, "Stick it up your ass and spin on it, brother dear. Say whatever'n hell I get good and goddamned ready to say. Of all people, ignorant piece of walkin', talkin', steamin' horse manure like you should know that."

Jennings Bugg flashed a mouthful of crooked, stained teeth at Longarm and Marshal Forbes. "Do forgive my foul-mouthed li'l sister, gents. Simply the product of a piss-poor upbringin'. House fulla hairy-legged brothers. Folks died when she 'uz a nubbin. 'Course neither of 'em people was worth damn anyway, so it didn't matter much when they passed. Shit, life were awful hard for this here poor girl."

Longarm ignored Bathsheba Bugg's filthy-mouthed response to her dumber-than-dirt brother and the family history. Knifed his gaze from one outlaw to the other as he said, "You actually lookin' for somethin', Jennings? Or did you just stop by to demonstrate to anyone within earshot of a field howitzer exactly what a four-hole country shitter sounds like when it has the power of speech?"

Bugg's head snapped back as though he'd suffered a rap across the mouth. Recovered, then spread his legs and hooked stubby thumbs over a fancy, hand-tooled pistol belt. The deliberately belligerent move was tempered somewhat by the fact that the noted gunman and well-known killer kept his hands out front and close to his hammered-silver belt buckle.

"Lookin' fer brother Charlie, if'n it's any of your fuckin' business, lawdog. This here jaybird of a city lawman says Charlie's done went and bit the big one. Bought the ranch. Got no more pulse than a hoe handle. Deader'n Santa Anna. Says as how the *good* fuckin' folk of Val Verde, Texas, done up and had a little necktie party for Charlie. Strung 'im up. Stretched his neck."

Hamp Forbes, who'd leaned as far away from Jennings Bugg as he could get in his reclining, swivel-seated banker's chair, said, "Saw to Charlie's interment myself, Mr. Bugg. Planted him day before yesterday. Was a right stinky job, too. Being as how he dangled from a tree limb for four or five days before I could get him down. But the city fathers of Val Verde did right by the man in death. Provided a coffin, local preacher read over him, had several paid mourners to see him off to the other side. Not sure any man could ask for much more."

From his corner, Fast Eddie Bloodsworth flipped his

bowie around like a twitching stinger, then snapped, "Why'n the hell'd it take so long to get Charlie down outta yer hangin' tree and into the ground in the first place, Forbes? Ain't right to leave a man danglin' like that far as I'm concerned, by God. Left out to the mercy or whims of man and nature like some kinda fuckin' animal kilt under the ironbound wheels of a passin' wagon. Ain't no wonder he stunk."

Forbes ran nervous fingers back and forth across the top of his desk, then stared at the back of one hand as though looking for just the right answer. After several seconds of silence passed, he said, "Well, there were some delicate considerations I had to take into account."

Bathsheba Bugg hopped to her feet, shook the quirt at Val Verde's marshal, and screeched, "What the hell does that mean? 'Delicate considerations.' What kinda bullshit you tryin' to shovel our fuckin' direction, Forbes?"

Appeared to Longarm that Hamp Forbes was about to run short of patience with all the questioning. The normally unperturbed city star toter brought his chair to an upright position with a resounding thump. He smacked the top of his desk with an open palm, then yelled, "Your stupid brother murdered one of Val Verde's most prominent citizens. A number of our most upstanding town folk witnessed that heinous crime. He even made good on his escape. But then, Marshal Long happened to bring him back through town, and the pent-up passions of some mighty good people momentarily overtook them."

"Well, that's the understatement of the year," Fast Eddy grumped from behind a lip-curling sneer.

Jennings Bugg turned away from Longarm. He pawed at a saddlebag, pistol belt, and small pile of other personal items sitting on one corner of Marshal Forbes's fancy desk. "You sure this here's all my brother's belongin's? Didn't find nothin' else?"

"Like what?" Longarm said.

Bugg glared at Longarm from the corner of one eye. "Money. Sizable sum of money, as a matter of pure fact. 'N maybe somethin' else as ain't none a yer fuckin' business, Long."

Longarm grinned. "Oh, there was *some* money when he was captured all right. Seems Charlie had possession of a tidy amount stolen during an express car robbery some weeks ago 'bout a hundred miles east of Denver. Money that belongs to the federal government of these United States. I aim to see what he had, and anything else I can recover, gets back into the hands of the right people. You folks don't by any chance have any more of the loot, do you?"

Heads of all three of Marshal Forbes's belligerent visitors snapped up at the same time. Bathsheba Bugg popped the quirt against the leg of her split-crotched leather riding skirt, then brought the abbreviated whip up and tapped it against her shoulder. "You accusin' us of somethin' there, Marshal Long?"

Longarm grinned. "Oh, no, ma'am. Wouldn't even consider such a bold-as-brass move without gold-plated proof."

Fast Eddy snorted, stepped out of his corner, then pushed the butts of his pistols forward with the backs of his arms. "You by any chance carryin' paper on any of us there, Marshal? Got wants, warrants, or such to serve?"

Longarm scratched his chin, then grinned at the girl. "Nope. Pure fact is I don't have a thing of real substance on any of you. Not as yet. But I will offer some advice."

"And what'd that be?" Bathsheba Bugg purred.

"Was me, miss, I'd saddle up and get the hell outta town just as quick as I could. See, I got all this damage to my face tryin' to protect your dumber'n-dirt brother. Can't imagine what the locals around here might be capable of once they discover just exactly who you folks are."

Jennings Bugg swelled up like a stomped-on toad frog. "Fuck 'em. Each and every one. We come and go whenever and wherever we please, Long. Right now, it pleases me for us to stick around town a spell. Think we'll take a room at that hotel we passed on the way in. Talk with anyone willing. Get a better perspective on things. 'Sides, I expect we're gonna insist that Charlie's body gets dug up."

For a second, Hamp Forbes looked as though he might puke up his breakfast. "Dug up? Are you actually crazier than a shit house rat?"

Bugg's eyes widened until a halo of white showed around each pupil and his neck turned purple. He shook a knotted finger in Forbes's face. "Dug up, by God. 'S what I jus' said, and 's what I meant. Disintered, exhumed, uncovered, unearthed. Want 'im outta the fuckin' ground so's I can search through his pockets and such."

Forbes flipped an agitated gesture at the pile on his desk. "As God is my witness, that's all he had. We didn't find anything else. And trust me, we looked."

Through gritted, yellow teeth, Bugg snarled, "Well, now, that's just the point. We don't trust any of you law-pushin' assholes. 'Sides, I might know some places to look as you didn't bother with."

Longarm choked back a snorting chuckle. "Now, that leaves an image in my brain I'd rather not think on too much."

"What the hell's that mean, Long?" Bugg yelped.

"Nothing. Nothing. Didn't mean a thing."

Forbes said, "Even if Doc Hughes, our local coroner, agreed to such an idiotic effort, you wouldn't find me out in the Mount Olive Cemetery with a shovel. For the love of God, you go and open your brother's grave and the stench would knock a buzzard off a shit wagon."

"You don't have to do anything, Marshal," Bathsheba Bugg offered. "We'll take care of the job ourselves."

Forbes threw a harried look at Longarm, as though seeking support. The Denver-based lawman simply rolled his eyes and shrugged.

Forbes said, "Don't know what you folks have in mind, and don't really care. But I'm warning you to leave the man in peace. Personally, can't imagine anything worse than messing around with ole Charlie's final resting place. Hell, he suffered through enough the last few minutes of his wretched life."

Bugg made a chopping motion of the hand at his companions. Entire trio started moving toward the jail's front door at the same time. The blue-eyed Bathsheba was the last one out. Sultry gal brushed so close to Longarm, he could smell her. Heavy odor of damp, ripe, gooey womanhood flooded his flared nostrils as she swayed by and, on the sly, winked at him.

My God, Longarm thought, girl's cooz must be juicer than an overripe Georgia peach. A bead of sweat as big as an Arkansas pecan ran down his cheek, then dripped off a clenched chin, as he watched Bathsheba's muscular, saddle-conditioned behind sway through the doorway and out onto the boardwalk. Gal's succulent, undulating ass resembled a couple of rambunctious kids wrestling under a patchwork blanket. Longarm's sweaty response as he eyed her shapely caboose was brought on by the distinct possibility there just might be more than a good chance for a bit of danger-tinged diddling sometime in the near future.

Hamp Forbes snatched Longarm's attention off Bathsheba Bugg's beautiful bum when he said, "You think those folks'll be a problem, Marshal Long?"

Custis Long strode to the chair Charlie Bugg's sister had recently abandoned and flopped into it. Snatched his hat off and fanned a flushed face. "Oh, hell, yes. 'Course they'll be a problem. All of 'em born to cause trouble, given just about any kind of piss-poor excuse. Their kind spends every waking hour of their lives looking for something to have a problem with, and you know it, Hamp. And, hell, good citizens of Val Verde have handed them just what they needed on a silver plate by stringin' ole Charlie up to the biggest live oak in this part of the state. Gonna be killings over this, Hamp. Just a matter of time."

"Was afraid you'd say something like that."

"You can bet the ranch on it. They're here to cause trouble—pure and simple. Was me, I'd send word out to the Tyler ranch that it'd be a good idea if none of that benighted bunch darkened a city street in Val Verde for a few days."

Forbes frowned and shook his head. "Doubt that suggestion's gonna set well with the Tylers. The whole bunch of them usually rides in almost every afternoon for a few drinks at Crabb's Saloon. Bugg's brother and sister happen to stroll into that joint looking for trouble, they're gonna get it—in spades."

Longarm scratched his jaw. "Maybe the Tylers should make it a point to stay out of town until a week or so after this bunch has taken their leave. 'S what I'd do."

"What you or I'd do, Marshal Long, doesn't mean spit to the Tyler family."

Longarm nodded. "I know. I know, you're right, Hamp. Personally, wish Jennings and the other two would take a hike, because I'd like to spend a few minutes alone with each and every one of 'em Tyler sonsabitches myself. Give 'em back a nice-sized helpin' of what's showin' on my face right now."

Obviously agitated, Forbes ran a shaky hand from forehead to chin as though tired all the way to the soles of his feet. "Any message to the Tyler bunch about staying out of town won't do a bit of good, Long. Fact is, it'd probably just make matters worse. You tell a headstrong son of a bitch like Jack Tyler not to do a thing, and he'll go right ahead and do it just to see how uncomfortable you get while you watch him disobey. Bet if I sent word out to the ranch, like you said, he'd be in town looking for trouble before my messenger could get turned around good and headed back."

Longarm picked at the irritating piece of curved leather and gauze covering his eye. Whole mess itched like hell's eternal, sulfurous blazes. More than just about anything he could think of, he wanted to rip the entire gob of crap off his face and throw it into the street.

Instead, the uncomfortable federal lawdog twisted his head around, threw Forbes his most thoughtful, one-eyed squint, and said, "The three people who just stomped out your door are more dangerous than any homegrown problem you've ever had around here, Hamp. This bunch makes the Tyler boys, and their mouthy sister, look like members of a Baptist church choir."

"Really think they're that bad, huh?"

"Any one of 'em would kill the two of us and not even bat an eye. Then kill off half the town to get whatever it is they're here for. Then burn the fuckin' town to the ground. Ride right through the ashes to get away."

"That gal, Bathsheba, gave you quite an eyeballing on the way out just now, Long. Think maybe she might have other plans for the two of you before she lets her brother put any bullet holes in your hide."

Longarm stood, slapped his hat back on, and headed for the door. Hesitated in the doorway, turned, then, almost as if to himself, said, "Now that I've thought on it a bit, sendin' word to the Tyler bunch might not be such a terrible idea after all. Yeah. Could be right interestin' to see what happens when these two clans of certifiable idiots butt heads."

A distinct look of horror flickered in Hamp Forbes's eyes. "I'm not looking forward to anything like that happening in my town."

Longarm nodded in agreement, then said, "Completely understandable. Appears inevitable, though."

"My ole pappy always said, 'Hamp, my boy, ain't nothin' inevitable.' "

"Well, in this particular case, think your ole pappy

mighta had to change his philosophy a bit. 'Less you wanna gut up and try to run Jennings, Bathsheba, and Fast Eddie out of town, there's killin's in our future."

"God above," Forbes groaned.

"Firmly believe as how it just might be best to go on ahead and bring this festerin' pimple to a head. Render that sucker out to gooey squz as soon as possible."

"Don't leave a cautious man much wiggle room, Long."

"Well, if what you say 'bout the Tylers is true, we probably won't have to wait very long for the bloodshed to get started. In the meantime, if you ain't gonna send 'em packin', just might wanna keep in mind that Bathsheba Bugg's bad and her brother's worse. But Fast Eddie Bloodsworth might well be the walking, talking equivalent of a diamondback rattler. Man can draw and shoot better'n anyone you've ever gone up against. Evil skunk ain't gonna die in bed, that's for damn sure. Should the need arise, and it will, wouldn't approach 'em with anything like brotherly love in my heart. Could well end up deader'n a gunnysack fulla coyote bait."

Chapter 11

Bubbling like a cauldron of liquid metal forced up from the earth's mysterious interior depths, a dull-orange sun squatted on the western horizon, like an angry, round, fire-belching gargoyle. Reddish light from the rapidly sinking orb flowed down Val Verde's main thoroughfare like volcanic lava. Heaven's moving glow bled onto the sandy soil east of town. Swept west, toward night, in waves of graduated gray. Turned into pale violet, then lilac, then deep purple. Finally, day turned into the pitch-black of darkness as it crept up the foothills of Indian, Military, and Turkey Mountains.

The shadows of businesses on either side of the street had lengthened and were rapidly creeping into the middle of the busy boulevard. Much to the entire town's relief, the evening had already cooled enough to allow some freedom of outside movement. Appeared as though almost every family for miles around had abandoned their stuffy homes for an evening stroll. Knots of smiling, laughing people gathered in companionable groups around benches outside the stores, shops, and saloons.

Longarm eased through the jailhouse doorway, pulled it shut, and stepped onto the boardwalk. He lingered in the veranda's expanding shadow just long enough to watch Jennings Bugg, the fiery Bathsheba, and Eddie Bloodsworth lead their animals down the street toward the Bishop

Hotel. In spite of the movement of so many other people on the street, the slow, rhythmic, clippety-clop of their mounts' iron-shod feet could still be heard all up and down the canyonlike thoroughfare.

Soon as the dangerous trio disappeared inside the town's only functioning inn, Longarm hobbled across Val Verde's stone-paved main street and headed for Doc Hughes's office. For some unfathomable reason, the busted-up lawdog's lower right leg had begun to hurt like hell. Hadn't bothered him before, but now a stabbing pain, from hip to knee, suddenly shot out of nowhere with such impact, he thought for a second he might well have to stop and take stock of the situation before going on. Shit, he thought, is it possible I'm in need of a cane like some old toothless geezer about ready for a sad death and a cold grave? He tried to shake off the pain and hastened his pace.

Fully expecting to find a panting Nettie Hughes buck-assed nekkid and waiting spread-eagle in his bed like an open book, he hobble-hustled through the infirmary's empty outer reception area. Wobbled down the office's hallway to his room, behind the last door on the right, then burst inside with all the pent-up fervor of an overexcited adolescent.

To his total surprise, and great disappointment, the room proved completely vacant. A darting glance flicked from one barren corner to the next, as if he expected to find his beautiful, passionate nurse crouched in one of them and trying to hide.

Once he'd admitted to himself that he might well have misinterpreted the girl's prior actions and words, Longarm pitched his hat onto the tiny dressing table next to the door. He limped to the bed, sat on the edge, and with some difficulty pushed his boots off. Hurt like hell, but after several minutes of torturous effort, he'd removed his pistol belt and all his clothing, carefully folded and stacked each piece of it in the seat of a nearby chair.

A protracted inspection of his right leg by way of the dressing table mirror revealed a massive, previously unnoticed, yellow-tinged, black-and-blue bruise on the back of the aching limb. The ugly discoloration extended along the exact area that hurt so painfully. Damned spot was shaped exactly like the sole of a man's pointy-toed, high-heeled boot.

He kneaded the injured muscles for several minutes with equally sore fingers. Puzzled a bit over why it hadn't bothered him at some point before. Then, dressed in nothing but his balbriggans, he fluffed both pillows into a downy stack and stretched out on the bed. Propped himself up to the point of almost sitting. The eye, and all the other blotchy contusions decorating his mutilated, stringy-muscled body, still ached like sulfurous hell itself. But, he had to admit, he wasn't in anywhere nearly as much pain as he had been a mere forty-eight hours prior.

Longarm closed his good eye and, before he knew it, drifted off to sleep.

Wicked visions of a naked Nettie Hughes, Billie Tyler, and Bathsheba Bugg flooded the sleeping lawman's unconscious, dreamy reveries with writhing bodies, heavy-nippled breasts, flared hips, and whispered entreaties for pulse-pounding sex. The heaving, constantly changing fantasy had barely got going good when the women appeared to somehow blend together, then separate into new, different, bizarrely changed forms. Nettie Hughes now had Bathsheba Bugg's waist-length black hair. Billie Tyler's green eyes had somehow turned a pale slate blue, and her sun-caressed face was milk white and almost ghostlike.

Just about the time he'd managed to get all three of those heavenly female visions totally unclothed and into the same bed at the same time, he snapped awake. Found himself staring into the face of a concerned-looking Nettie Hughes. She sat on the edge of the bed, a firm, shapely hip pressed against his. One of her hands lay on the shoulder nearest his patched eye. He could feel the pulsating heat flowing from her body at every point of contact between them. Once again, her gaze was locked on the enormous, thickened, rigid, sausagelike lump that originated at the juncture of his thighs and crept up almost to the waistband of his drawers.

With considerable effort, she appeared to tear attention away from the object of her obvious interest. "I-I-I had hoped to be here when you returned. Unfortunately, my father was called out of town again," she said, then knifed another fleeting glimpse at Longarm's rigid prong. "Had to help him prepare for the trip."

"Oh, I understand completely."

As though suddenly realizing she might have been caught red-handed doing something naughty, Nettie's gaze snapped back up to Longarm's face as she said, "Before leaving, Father did say it would be all right to remove the patch and bandage over your eye."

"Well, you just can't imagine how good it is to hear that. 'Specially after my visit with that bunch in Hamp's office this afternoon. Gonna need both of my eyes if those folks get frisky."

Nettie lifted the leather covering away from Longarm's puffy swollen eye, then said, "Papa recommended that if the wound has not deteriorated in any substantial way, might be the best idea all around for us to leave the dressing off so some fresh air can get to it."

A pleased grin played across Custis Long's cracked, scab-covered lips. "Sounds good to me."

She dropped the leather patch into a metal tray sitting atop the nightstand next to his bed. "Hold still and don't open the eye until I tell you," she said, then took a set of scissor-shaped tweezers from the tray. She leaned over until the side of one breast was pressed against his unyielding root and began lifting the pads of gauze away from the wound, one thin layer at a time.

Longarm shifted the lower half of his body. Nettie leaned more of her weight, and breast, against him, as though to keep him from moving about. Though still one-eyed, he couldn't help but notice that the girl appeared to thoroughly enjoy having the crowbar in his balbriggans pressed beneath her arm and against the weight of her breast. She would lean forward, pick at the bandage, then lean away to dispose of it. All the while the smiling woman kept up the rubbing pressure against his anvil-hard doniker.

After what seemed to Longarm like an eternity of being picked at, pressed against, and rubbed into a near frenzy, Nettie chirped, "All right, you can open up now."

He tried, but nothing happened.

"Wait, wait just another second," she said. "I think we might need to soak it with a bit of water. Your lashes appear stuck together."

Several minutes later, she gently dabbed at the wound with a damp rag for one last time, then said, "Now, try again."

Longarm's eye popped open, then quickly closed. He held a hand up to shade against the dying light outside his room's only window, then blinked the aching orb open again.

"Can you see? How many fingers am I holding up, Custis?"

"'S a bit foggy, Nettie, but I pert sure there's two of 'em."

A relieved laugh popped from between the girl's comely lips. "That's wonderful. Couldn't be better, as a matter of pure fact. Must admit, I did have my fears. Here," she said, and held out the handle of a woman's dressing-table mirror about the size of a dinner plate. "Take a look."

He brought the reflective glass as close to his injured face as he could. Searched the still-bruised and blackened cheek and socket for anything that resembled permanent damage. "'S a bit better'n the last time I got a peek at this mess in the mirror over yonder by the wall. But it still hurts some."

"Maybe I can help relieve a bit of the pain," Nettie Hughes said, then grabbed the waistband of his cotton underwear and jerked down.

The tip of Longarm's pulsating dong popped out. Nettie grabbed his saber-stiff tool with trembling fingers, then quickly covered the thick tip with hot, slurping-wet kisses. Then her mouth engulfed and flowed over the thick knob like a wave of heated honey.

Longarm groaned with pent-up pleasure as a tongue of fleshy flame darted round and round the bulbous stalk's pointed apex. Knowledgeable beyond anything he could have expected, she paid particular sucking attention to the edges of the blood-engorged cap on his throbbing root. Erect tingling nerve ends protruded there like tiny white fingers.

The panting girl brought her head up and hissed, "Lord forgive me, but I get so worked up when a man displays this kind of excitement from just looking at me." Grinning, she again slid as much of him into her steamy mouth as she could, then sucked all the way off with a resounding pop. "And God above, but I do love having one of these things in my mouth."

Longarm dropped the mirror into the bedsheets. Arched his sore back, then ran aching fingers into the silken mat of Nettie's hair. Then, as gently as urgency allowed, he urged her greedy mouth back onto his unbending tool again.

The enthusiastic woman went at his prong with gleeful relish. Stabbed at the eyelike slit in the tip with her tongue, then slid stretched lips over the shaft and pulled on his stiff prick with unparalleled vigor.

After being at her amorous task for several minutes, she suddenly stopped, held his thick love muscle in one hand, rubbed it against her cheek, and said, "You can spurt if you want, Custis. I know some women don't like it when a man really cuts loose—but I do. Simply love the taste of a man. All of him."

With that, she jerked his underpants down over his hips, then shoved them to his knees. Nosed his balls aside, licked the skin beneath, then sucked the tender, sensitive flesh up with nibbling lips. At the same time, she slid one hand up and down the steely shaft of his penis, while moaning like a female mountain lion in heat.

After almost half an hour of energetic oral exertion, Nettie Hughes appeared to decide that her incredibly well-endowed partner just might need a bit more in the way of heated stimulation. She hopped to her feet, stood, and began snatching clothing from her ripe, needy body. Once completely naked, she indulged in a performance specifically designed to further arouse his already inflamed desire.

Longarm watched as Nettie ran one hand down her board-flat belly to a mound of Venus covered with a patch of amazingly long corn-silk-colored hair. She boldly spread the rosy-pink treasure hidden there with her fingers. Gasped as she petted the exposed, glistening gash with one hand, while rubbing and pinching erect nipples, the size of the last joint on a grown man's finger, with the other. At one point, the panting girl locked him in a sweaty, hot-eyed gaze, lifted each magnificent, cone-shaped breast, and lovingly sucked her own already erect nipples.

With those magnificent boobs dangling against his lips, she climbed back onto the bed, threw a leg over Longarm's waiting body, then grabbed his turgid dingus and guided it into her gushing nook.

Took some effort, but Nettie Hughes managed to slide every broad, thickened inch of Longarm's colossal pecker into her glistening, fiery cooz. Once he'd finally hit bottom, she grabbed one of the turned dowels of the bed's decorative headboard in each hand and slowly began rocking back and forth.

"You don't have to move," she hissed. "I'll do all the work. Just hold still, hang on, and enjoy the ride."

Longarm smiled, put his hands behind his head, and took in as much of the spectacle going on between his legs as possible. In no time at all, a sheath of Nettie's glossy joy juice engulfed his rifle barrel of a prick. Eventually, the sticky, steamy fluid covered all the hair surrounding his cock and balls.

Nettie soon abandoned the rocking motion. She pushed away from the bed's headboard, came upright, and began to bounce up and down with wild abandon. She pounded her glorious quim against him with a rigorous intensity unlike any he'd experienced in some time. Nigh on every downward plunge of her flushed body resulted in an explosive, luscious orgasm.

Then, of a sudden, she rose straight up, as though hit by lightning. Did a complete about-face on his iron-hard tool and grabbed his ankles. The view of her lush, pumping buttocks and gushing pink gash spurred Longarm to heights of performance he could hardly believe, given his battered condition. And when it appeared his energetic lover was well on the way to totally exhausting herself, he grabbed the moaning Nettie by the ass, rolled the sex-addled girl onto her back, crawled up between her legs, and took control of the situation.

No need for anything like a buildup. He started his energetic thrusting at top speed. In the blink of an eye, he was pounding into her creamy depths like the pushrod on a Mississippi River stern-wheeler.

At one point, it appeared as though Nettie's eyes rolled into the back of her head. For several seconds, Longarm could see only fluttering eyelids and the exposed whites. Then she recovered, locked her heels together at the small of his back, darted a hand down between their sweat-and sex-drenched bodies, found the perfect, nubby spot, and used three fingers to rub herself frantic.

Of a sudden, their frenetic lovemaking turned into something totally different. Nettie pushed Longarm away, then quickly rolled onto her stomach. Head buried in the pillows, she drew onto her knees and raised her beautiful ass. The target proved too much to resist. Longarm grabbed the moaning woman's arms and pulled them back and toward him for maximum leverage. He held her by the wrists and plunged into her squirting, luscious snatch. Brought his hips upward with such force, Nettie squeaked and wiggled against his invading tool as he bounced the squealing girl near a foot in the air and into an orgasmic crescendo.

Took several more minutes for the sated Nettie to stop bucking on the end of Longarm's still-turgid cock. He stayed with her, matched every subtle movement, even redoubled his efforts until she could no longer move. Then, nigh on exhausted, the panting lawman rolled onto his side and lay with his motionless partner's legs draped over the lower half of a sweat-saturated body.

After a few minutes of much-needed recovery, Longarm pried himself from beneath Nettie's sleep-heavy form, then strode to his stack of clothing. Fished out a fresh cheroot. Stoked the rum-soaked tobacco to life, then eased over to the room's open window. Night breeze felt mighty good as it washed across tired, knotted muscles. And while he would have had to admit, if asked, that he felt like warmed-over hell on a pitchfork, his bout with the lovely Nettie had been exactly what he needed.

The slumping deputy U.S. marshal had almost finished his smoke when he heard faint movement in the bed at his back. He turned and gazed into the darkness. Took a second for tired eyes to focus before he could see Nettie's pleasing shape against the tangle of damp sheets.

Propped against the pillows, the insatiable woman spread her legs, held her arms out, and said, "Come back to bed, Custis. Papa won't be back until sometime tomorrow afternoon."

He flicked the cigar stub out the window, turned, and fell into the bed. Landed with his head between her raised legs. She giggled when he said, "'Pears this is gonna be a longer night than I thought."

Nettie ran her fingers into his hair, then pulled his face into her gooey, waiting muff. "Yes, much longer," she moaned. "Oh, oh, oh, my God. Do that again. Ummmm, right there. Deep. Stick your tongue in as deep as you can. Oh, yes. Yes indeed."

Chapter 12

Next morning, having tried with no success to rouse a sated, uncooperative Nettie Hughes for breakfast, a bleary-eyed Deputy U.S. Marshal Custis Long sipped at a steaming cup of the finest coffee he'd tasted in years while sitting alone at a corner table in the Bishop Hotel's restaurant. He had very deliberately selected that particular spot to park himself because it offered the ever-inquisitive lawman the widest possible view of Val Verde's main street—especially the entrance to Hamp Forbes's office.

An empty plate waited on the table at Longarm's elbow for the server to take away. Only minutes before, the spotless dish had been loaded with scrambled eggs, half a dozen feather-light soda biscuits drenched in a gob of sawmill gravy, along with piles of bacon and fried sausage. Now there remained not a single crumb.

On the sly, the sleep-deprived lawdog dropped one hand beneath the table. Gently rubbed his aching tool, then pulled out a nickel cheroot. "Woman came damned near to killin' me last night," he mumbled, then scratched a lucifer to life, but stopped short while in the process of putting flame to the cigar. With the smoldering match hovering near his face like a small sun, he glanced out the window onto the near-deserted main thoroughfare. Couldn't help but notice what appeared to be an agitated citizen stutter-stepping his way toward the marshal's fancified office and iron-barred jail.

Longarm shook the shortened lucifer to death before it could singe his fingers, then flicked it onto the floor. Bearded, shabby-dressed, and wizened-looking in a kind of broken-down, ill-kept, desert-rat way, the old man in the street led a heavily loaded burro. Hawk-faced, deeply tanned in all the areas of his face not covered by a scruffy white beard, he took a few jerky, hesitant steps. Stopped. Talked to himself for some seconds, then started off again while still conversing with the air and the empty street at large. Stopped again. Chatted with the sky, ground, or his feet, then struck out once more. Came to an abrupt halt, whispered something into the burro's ear, then suddenly got in a hurry.

With his lawman's inquisitive gaze glued onto the strange-acting geezer, Longarm stood, placed coins on the table next to his plate, shoved his snuff-colored Stetson on, then hurried for the street. On the boardwalk, he took time enough to light his cigar while watching as the codger tied the burro to the hitch rack out front of the marshal's office, then disappeared through Hamp Forbes's front door.

No more than ten seconds behind the bearded old fogy, Longarm stepped across the Val Verde marshal's threshold just in time to hear Forbes say, "I don't have the time, or the patience, for this kind of total bullshit right now. Swear to Jesus, Willie, if this is nothing more than another one of your tall tales, take an oath on my sainted mother's grave I'll throw you in a cell out back and keep you there for a month."

Old-timer glanced around at Longarm, as though somewhat startled by his entrance, then jerked an agitated gaze back onto Forbes and clamped his mouth shut.

Forbes, standing rather than sitting, leaned against the gun rack behind his desk and said, "Nothing to fear. He's a U.S. marshal, Willie. Now, slow down. Take your time. Tell me the whole lunatic tale. Don't leave anything out."

Old coot shook a dirty-nailed, knotted finger in Longarm's direction. "You sure 'bout that 'un, Hamp? Don't look much like no U.S. lawman as I ever seen. Looks to 've been whipped on right smart, you ask me. Ain't sayin' nothin' else 'less you can garn-tee he ain't somebody'll kill me deader'n a rotten stump."

In spite of himself, an amused smile spread across Longarm's bruised and scratch-covered, scab-decorated face.

Forbes shook his head like a tired bloodhound, flopped back into his banker's chair, and stared at the ceiling as if guidance might float down from the rafters overhead. "He's a deputy U.S. marshal, Willie. Please, say hello to Willie Stayton, Marshal Long."

Longarm tipped his hat. "Mr. Stayton."

Willie Stayton appeared to make an effort at speaking. His lips moved, but nothing came out.

"Get on with it, Willie, or I swear to crucified Jesus I'm going to throw you in the hoosegow," Forbes said.

Stayton's face twisted into a mask of personal hurt and feigned pain. "You know how I hate bein' locked up, Hamp."

"Yes, I do," Forbes muttered. "And that's exactly why I'm running out of patience. Now go over the entire song and dance again. Keep it slow. Try not to garble everything up, or go to jabbering like a loon the way you did when you rushed in here. Still not exactly sure what in the blue-eyed hell you said."

Squint-eyed and suddenly taking on the appearance of a cornered rat, the dust-covered Willy Stayton glared at Longarm one more time, then turned back to Marshal Forbes and said, "Christ on a crutch, takes me a month to get over one day in your lockup and you know it, Hamp."

"You going to tell me why you burst into my office or not, Willie?"

"Well, yeah. Like I done said afore this runnin' buddy a yern interrupted me, I 'uz down to Pandale visitin' friends of mine last week. Coming back into town along the Pecos Road. Like I always do. Took a trail off'n the road so's I didn't have to walk an extra half mile. Mile and a half or so out yonder where the road curves back to the west, you know the spot. You know's well's I do, 'at 'ere path leads right through the graveyard. Me'n Maybell foller'd 'er on in."

"Don't tell me," Longarm said. "You found an open grave."

Willy Stayton glared at Longarm as though he had just found a scorpion in his boot. Old-timer sounded taken aback when he said, "Yeah. Sure 'nuff did, mister." Then he slowly turned back to Hamp Forbes and added, "Stinkin' corpse was a-layin' atop a pile of shoveled-up dirt. Right next to the open grave, Hamp. Poor, putrid sunnamabitch waddn't even in his hole like he's a 'sposed to be. Somethin' of a surprisin' sight, don't you think? Thought fer a second 'er two as how maybe he'd done went and kicked the dirt up and crawled out by hisself. Give me a case of the tremblin' spooks. Come nigh on to havin' a stroke."

"You recognize the dead man, Willie?" Longarm said.

"Nope. Cain't say as I did. Marker had the name Charlie Bugg on it. Figure he had to be the one. 'Peared to me as how Mr. Bugg done been in the ground a few days 'fore I found 'im a-layin' there like that. Putrefied and damned stinky, you see. Black in the face and all. Pretty much festerated up and such. Missin' at least one eye. Looked like birds had been at 'im as well, you ask me. Not sure I'd a recognized my own pappy in the kinda state that unfortunate wretch were in."

Forbes shook his head, rubbed at a scratched spot atop his desk with a fingertip dampened with spit, then said, "Don't suppose you bothered to put the poor, dead, unfortunate bastard back in the ground, did you?"

Stayton tapped the top of Forbes's fancy banker's desk with the knuckles of one hand, as though knocking on the door of an empty house. "Well, now, I thunk 'bout it,

Hamp. Yeah. I surely thunk about it. Most assuredly done 'at. Even started out to put 'im back, but I didn't see no box as he coulda come out of. Figured the poor feller's coffin had to still be in the ground. Either that 'er some skunk musta gone an' stole it. Couldn't believe that, though. Mean, who'd go an' steal a dead feller's casket?"

Longarm eased from his spot next to the door to one of the guest chairs against the wall opposite Hamp Forbes's desk. Said, "So, Willie, say you did give some thought to puttin' the corpse back in the ground?"

Willie Stayton appeared uncomfortable with Custis Long sitting behind him. The nervous, toothless gummer moved to the end of the city marshal's desk nearest the barred entrance of the jail's cell block in an apparent effort to keep both lawmen in easy view. "Yep. I thunk on it. Sure did."

"But you didn't. Why not?" Longarm said.

Stayton glanced from one badge toter to the other, then said, "'Cause, Mr. Smart-assed U.S. Lawman, didn't care fer the smell fer one thang. But worse 'n that, kinda snuck up an' took a gander down in at 'ere fuckin' hole and, glory be to God, they 'uz already another feller down 'ere."

"What?" Longarm and Forbes said at the same time.

"Swear to Jesus, boys. Laid out in the coffin like an undertaker done put 'im down 'ere. Hands acrost his chest, like he's a-waitin' fer words to be read over 'im. Ready to have dirt clods slung on top of 'im."

Longarm flinched.

Forbes moaned.

"Yeah. Know how you boys feel," Willie Stayton continued. "Damnedest thang I've seen since my days a-fightin' them Northern devils durin' Mr. Lincoln's War of Yankee Aggression on the Glorious South. Witnessed some horrible shit back then, boys. Helped bury thousands of bodies at a time back in them days. Unspeakable. Jus' ghastly stuff. Ain't seen nothin' like it since then. Don't wanna hafta to see nothin' like it again. But findin' these two corpses at the same time come damned close."

"We understand, Willy," Hamp Forbes snapped. "But you're getting off the subject."

"Sorry. But ain't often a man walkin' along mindin' his own business finds a dead feller a-layin' on the side of an open grave. And another feller a stretched out in the coffin at the bottom of a hole what has all the dirt tossed out. Leastways, sure'n hell beats anythang as I've seen lately."

Hamp Forbes stared at his hands like a man who would have given just about anything to be somewhere else. "Sweet Jesus," he muttered. "You by any chance recognize the poor bastard in the coffin, Willie?"

"Yeah. Sure 'nuff. 'Course I did."

Several seconds passed. Stayton appeared to have run out his string and didn't have anything else to offer.

After a prolonged silence, Longarm said, "Well, out with it, Willie. Who'd you see in the coffin? Certain Marshal Forbes is just like me. We'd sure as hell like to know who you found. Wouldn't we, Hamp?"

Forbes groaned and rubbed a thick vein, pulsing at his temple. "Well, yeah, Willie. Would be kind of nice to know who the dead feller was that you found at the bottom of an open grave, being as how we should have only one fairly fresh corpse lurking around out in the graveyard right now. Give it up. Tell us. Who was it?"

Willie Stayton's heavily tanned face appeared to go white. "Pert sure it 'uz Wade Tyler, Hamp. You know, the big, dumb one a them Tyler boys? Big bastard had a bullet hole right 'twixt the eyes. 'Course, when you're sportin' a head size of that boy's fifty-pound punkin of a noggin, makes for a damned fine target, I suppose."

Hamp Forbes looked stricken, then leaned toward Stayton. "Sweet Jesus. You're certain about all this, Willie? No doubt the man in the grave was Wade Tyler? Not a single question in your mind?"

"Nope. It 'uz Wade all right. Known that big ole kid mosta his life. 'Course when I realized it were him, 'at 'ere sure 'nuff scared the bejabberous snot outta me. You imagine the hell there's gonna be to pay when his brothers, Jack and Drew, find out 'bout this, Hamp? Them boys gonna come to Val Verde lookin' to rip somebody a new asshole. Maybe even rip the whole town a new one."

Stretched out in his chair, with legs crossed at the ankle and appearing steeped in thought, Longram laid interlaced fingers atop the buckle of his pistol belt. Said, "Don't think we'll have to look far to find those responsible for this killin', Hamp."

Forbes closed his eyes, pinched the bridge of his nose, then groaned. "Jennings Bugg and Fast Eddie Bloodsworth."

Longarm nodded. "Yep. One or the other, but most probably, both of 'em. Girl might even have had a hand in it, too."

Forbes made a shooing motion at Stayton. "Get on out of here, Willie. We'll take care of Wade. Inform his family and such. No need for you to stick around. Besides, Marshal Long and I have important things to talk over."

Stayton nodded. Headed for the door, but stopped in the open entryway. Said, "'Spose you don't want me tellin' nobody 'bout this here dance, do ya, Hamp?"

"You suppose right, Willie. Need to keep this under your hat until we can talk it all over with the Tyler family."

The geezer hit the office entry as fast as a man his age could trundle out. Slammed the heavy door so hard as he departed, sounded like a pistol shot.

Longarm shifted in the chair, then leaned forward with his arms crossed atop his knees. "Haven't really noticed before, Hamp, but I'm guessin' you folks do have an undertaker stashed 'round here somewhere."

"Sure. Hiram Dobson. Man of many parts. Owns the mercantile and furniture businesses over yonder across the street. Also has a barbering setup in one corner of the store. And he's Val Verde's lone undertaker. Doesn't put a sign out or anything. Not in the man's makeup to advertise for such a service—or so he says."

"Gonna need a coffin to bring Tyler back in."

"Hiram also employs a carpenter who builds coffins out back of the store. Guess we might as well stroll on over there. Borrow Hiram's wagon. Pick up Pinky Caldwell and a casket. Go retrieve Wade Tyler's body."

A fleeting look of puzzlement flashed across Longarm's face. "Who's Pinky Caldwell?"

"Town's resident gravedigger. Figure as how somebody will have to put Charlie Bugg back in his hole and cover him up."

Longarm pushed up from the chair, squared his hat, then said, "Yeah, yeah, guess you're right. 'S a hellacious thought, but the job ain't gonna get done with us just sittin' here jawin' 'bout it."

Chapter 13

Longarm stood beside Charlie Bugg's open grave. Fished a bandanna from a hip pocket, then tied it around his sweating face bank-robber style. The odious, fetid scene looked pretty much exactly as described by Willie Stayton, but stank far more than a living body could have imagined. Poor Charlie Bugg's eyeless, decaying corpse lay atop a mound of fresh-dug earth piled next to the gaping hole in the ground. Wade Tyler's now-bloated body rested inside the coffin below, face to the sun, eyes open, staring up at passing clouds.

"Ever come on a scene to match this one, Long?" Hamp Forbes said from behind the protection of his own colorful nose cover. Val Verde's lawman shook his head in disgust, then added, "I sure as hell haven't. Been marshaling now for going on ten years. This nightmare flat beats all."

Longarm shrugged, as though bereft of words to describe the macabre scene. The ghoulish setting simply defied any sane man's ability to understand it.

Dressed in run-down brogans, grease-encrusted sailcloth pants, baggy linsey-woolsey shirt, and wearing a snap-brimmed tweed cap, Pinky Caldwell leaned on the handle of his shovel. He loafed near the feet of the fly-covered, malodorous remains of a rapidly decomposing Charlie Bugg, and gummed on a wad of cut plug the size of a duck egg.

A stream of tobacco juice squirted from Caldwell's toothless mouth. Slimy glob of spit dropped at the edge of the pile of clods beneath the outlaw's putrescent body. Scruffy gravedigger wiped dripping, stained lips on the sleeve of his shirt.

Before Longarm could respond to Hamp Forbes's question, Caldwell shook his head, then said, "Don't know 'bout yer friend, Marshal Forbes, but have to confess I can bear witness to more'n my share of some mighty strange happenings, along with large dollops of belligerent and downright rude behavior when it comes to burials, funerals, and the reopenin' of graves."

"I can just imagine," Forbes said.

"Doubt that, Hamp. But you can trust me when I say that I've known people to do some mighty strange shit before, durin', and after what should be a right solemn occasion."

"You must be working a different kind of interment service than any I've attended over the years, Mr. Caldwell," Longarm said.

Caldwell shook his head as though to indicate that Longarm had not a clue as to what he was talking about. Flashed a toothless, tobacco-dribbling grin, then spit again. "Dug a hole fer a feller several years ago over in Del Rio. Waitin' to fill 'er back up. 'Fore the preacher could even get finished with the service, family set the fur to flyin' in one helluva cussin' and spittin' contest. People went to yellin'. Fists went to bouncin' off'n folks' noggins. Blood, tears, and snot went to flyin'. Helluva hoedown. That bunch raised so much dust, Noah's little cloudburst couldn'a settled it."

"Jesus," Longarm muttered behind his mask.

"Yeah. Half a dozen of 'em red-eyed loons ended up down in the grave a-fightin' like a pack a turpentined wildcats. Can you believe it? Top of the coffin, what wasn't much more'n a single layer a pine planks nailed together, busted from all the weight, don't you know. Poor feller inside the box damn nigh got stomped all to pieces 'fore saner folk took control of the sitch-i-ation and the gruesome dance finally got brought to an end."

Forbes stared down into the hole at Wade Tyler's remains. Mumbled, "Incredible. Just by God incredible. Looks to have a dozen holes in his chest. Pure fact is there'll be bloody hell to pay when news of this killing gets back to the remaining Tylers."

Caldwell appeared not to have heard Marshal Forbes's telling observation, and plunged on with his recitation. "Was a humdinger of a dance all right. 'Course I've seen some funny ones, too. Hired out for a service over in Sonora some years ago. Come up a cloud 'bout the time the hearse was makin' its way from the church to the graveyard. Went to rainin' like a sunuvabitch. Turned into a real toad strangler. Put a foot of water in that grave faster'n you can spit. Still comin' down when the pallbearers brought the box up. Somebody went and lost his footin', don'cha know. Whole buryin' party ended up in the grave at the same time. Like to 've never got all them folks outta that hole. One feller ended up under the casket somehow. Damn near drowned. Figured as how that particular burying beat all I'd ever have to witness in this here profession. Helluva sight, that's fer damned sure. Have to admit, though, neither of them events as I've described fer you boys was nothin' compared to this mess."

Longarm held the bandanna close to his face. Bent over for a better view into the open hole in the ground. Then traced a line from the grave to Charlie Bugg's reeking carcass with his finger. "Looks to me like they dug ole Charlie up. Busted his box open. Then somebody tied a piece of rope around his ankles and just dragged him out."

Caldwell, who didn't appear bothered in the least by the eye-watering stench, torqued his scruffy head to one side like an inquisitive puppy. Said, "Whoever done 'er didn't wanna touch 'im. See. Cut all his pockets open. Notice that? Yeah. Bet the ranch whoever done this foul fuckin' deed didn't want to lay hands on that glob a oozin' rot. 'Course, I cain't blame 'em much. Poor sunuvabitch is mighty ripe. Gonna split open like a jellified sack of steamin' puss right soon. Hooo, wee, he'll really put out some stink then. Best get 'im back in the ground pronto."

"How long do you figure it would've taken for two men to dig ole Charlie up, Pinky?" Forbes said.

Caldwell scratched a stubble-covered chin. Flicked a bead of sweat from his dripping nose, then said, "Aw, given as how the ground was already nice and loose from me a-buryin' 'im the first time—jus' a few days ago, I might add. And given as how I only put 'im down about four feet to begin with—'cause the ground was harder'n the hubs of perdition, you see. Oh, prolly wouldna took more'n thirty minutes, I'd wager, Hamp. 'Bout the same amount of time it'd take a professional feller like me to do the dance alone."

Forbes eyed Custis Long and said, "We both know this had to have been the work of Bugg's recently arrived kinfolk. Evil sons of bitches apprised us of their intentions in no uncertain terms, and pretty much told us they were bound to do the foul deed, even if it harelips every angel in heaven."

Longarm nodded. "No doubt a'tall, they were lookin' for somethin'. A map. A note. Anything that mighta told 'em where the rest of the money they stole is. Be willin' to bet Jennings, Fast Eddie, and Bathsheba entrusted the bulk of the loot with Charlie after they robbed the express car out east of Denver. Little doubt in my mind he hid most of it. Then I caught up with him in Buckhorn and confiscated what was left over. Now they're screwed. He's deader'n a rotten hoe handle, and the money's gone. 'Cept for the bit I recovered. Bet ole Jennings is madder'n a jug of red ants 'bout now."

Hamp Forbes turned away from Charlie Bugg's reeking

corpse. Stumbled backward several steps. Took a number of deep, ragged breaths, then said, "Theory sounds about as good as any to me, Long. Well, let's go ahead and get Wade up out of the grave. Rebury ole Charlie. Then get the hell out of here. Not sure I can stand too much more of this smell."

Pinky Caldwell stabbed his shovel into the loose mound of dirt Bugg's corpse lay on, then hopped into the open grave. Longarm pitched a piece of rope down. Then he and Forbes watched as the gravedigger looped it around Wade Tyler's ankles.

For about ten minutes, the three men tried but couldn't pull the massive stiff out of the hole. Finally, a grinning Pinky Caldwell mopped a sweaty face on his sleeve, slapped his hat against one leg, and said, "Only one way to handle the big sunuvabitch boys."

He scrambled out of the hole. Tied the length of rope to the back of Hiram Dobson's wagon. Hopped into the cart's unpadded seat, switched the horse, and snatched Tyler out of the ground like a kid's corn-shuck doll.

"Easy as eatin' pie," Caldwell said as he climbed down, then strolled around the now-empty grave and used his shovel to lever Charlie Bugg back where he belonged. Corpse hit the bottom of the grave like a bagful of fire-cured Austin bricks.

Hamp Forbes grimaced, then shook a pointing finger at the rather awkward disposition of Charlie Bugg's much abused corpse. "Landed on his stomach, Pinky."

Caldwell grinned, then rocketed another glob of tobacco juice into the dust at his feet. "Doubt he'll mind much. Don't hear 'im complainin', do you? 'Sides, Hamp, 'less you wanna climb down there and turn 'im over, that's the way he's gonna stay."

Wade Tyler's corpse was delivered into the care of Hiram Dobson for embalming. Longarm made arrangements for a messenger to inform the family of the man's unfortunate passing. Then he and Hamp Forbes headed back to the marshal's office. The tired federal lawdog took his seat next to the wall. Slouched down into the chair. Leisurely crossed his legs at the ankles. Pulled a nickel cheroot, then stoked it to life and struck a thoughtful, troubled pose.

Forbes flopped into the squeaky banker's chair behind his desk. Leaned both elbows onto the polished top and propped his head in his hands. Sounded tired to the bone when he said, "You know, Long, can't say I'm all that surprised by this turn of events. Should've known something horrible was coming."

"No way to ever tell for sure with people like these, Hamp. Hell, they coulda vanished from the scene just as easily as they showed up."

"Yeah, well, during my evening patrol after you left yesterday, discovered from some of the local imbibers as how Jennings Bugg and Fast Eddie had set up shop over across the street in Bucky Crabb's drink-slinging emporium."

Longarm blew a satisfying cloud of gunmetal blue smoke toward the ceiling. Said, "Just exactly what you feared most. Huh, Hamp?"

"Belly-slinking snakes couldn't have picked a worse place. Unless they meant to do it a purpose, of course. Feel like I should have known, but still have trouble believing the bastards were so bold."

"Oh, if nothing else, the Bugg bunch is bold as brass."

"Tell you the truth, Custis. Now that I've had some time to think on it, I'm more than a bit surprised it didn't take those two skunks any longer than it did to ferret out where the Tyler bunch liked to hang out and spend their time drinking and gambling when they're in town. Which is damn near every afternoon that rolls around. Something of an oddity that Wade came in alone. Bet he strolled in for his afternoon taste, and Jennings and Fast Eddie figured out who he was. Bided their time. Waited till he was nigh on to knee-walking drunk, which was his usual practice, then waylaid the big bastard once he was in the process of heading for home."

Longarm nodded. "Sounds plausible to me. Good a theory as any." He pushed himself out of the chair. Pulled the Colt Lightning resting against his left side and flipped the loading gate open. Eyed each charged chamber, then slipped the weapon back into its oiled holster.

"What are you up to, Long?" Forbes said.

"Given our suspicions, think maybe we should stroll on over to Crabb's waterin' hole. See what we can find out. If we run on Jennings and Fast Eddie, might as well brace 'em on the spot. Light a fire under 'em. Twist their arms a bit. See what they say 'bout the shit storm that's gonna hit when the rest of the Tyler clan finds out 'bout their brother gettin' rudely rubbed out."

Forbes came to his feet with all the enthusiasm of a condemned man atop a scaffold awaiting his date with a hooded hangman. Turned and pulled a short-barreled shotgun from his weapons rack. "Might as well take one of my big blasters along. Sure wouldn't want Jennings or Fast Eddie to go and get too nervy."

Val Verde's anxious lawdog followed one step behind Longarm all the way to the bloodred batwings of Crabb's Big River Saloon. Both men drew up a step from the swinging café doors and peered inside.

To Longarm's surprise, the rough, sun-bleached board-and-batten exterior of Crabb's belied its gussied-up core. A dramatic fancy-carved, forty-foot, shellacked mahogany bar—topped with a slab of lustrous, gray black marble—ran along the entire length of the wall on his right. Matching back bar, stocked to the hilt with an amazing array of liquor selections, was highlighted by a gleaming mirror of equal length. A polished brass foot rail, as big around as a grown man's arm, surrounded the entire serving station. Six felt-covered poker tables, across an open space at least three steps from the bar, decorated the entire left side of the deep, oblong space.

An army of sparkling spittoons was strategically stationed every few feet around and about the glistening hardwood floors of the cow-country oasis. Resembled squatty golden soldiers standing at attention. A double-wide, doorless archway in the back wall opened onto an even larger area reserved for various kinds of house-sponsored table games. Longarm spied an idle roulette wheel and several pool tables on the other side of the opening.

Forbes leaned closer to Longarm and said, "Bit odd. This time of day, there's usually already a small crowd gathered here for the free sandwiches Bucky puts out every day."

A lone drink slinger stood behind the bar polishing glassware with a piece of damp bar rag as though his life depended on it. In the farthest corner near an unused, upright piano, Jennings Bugg and Fast Eddie Bloodsworth sat and smoked. To even the most casual observer, it would have appeared as how, on that particular morning, Bugg and Bloodsworth were the Big River's sole and only customers.

Longarm pushed through the batwings, took two steps over the threshold, then paused and waited for Marshal Forbes to catch up. Soon as he felt Val Verde's shotgun-carrying lawman near at his elbow again, Longarm strode directly for Jennings Bugg's newly established lair. Neither of the dangerous pair of gunnies at the table deigned to acknowledge the badge-wearing men as they approached.

Longarm drew up a few steps from the table, then flicked a finger that motioned Hamp Forbes around to his left. Pushed back on two legs, Jennings Bugg had his chair lodged as far into the corner as it would go. A holstered, bone-gripped pistol lay across his belly, and he stroked the weapon as though it were a living thing.

A grim-faced Fast Eddie Bloodsworth occupied the seat on his friend's immediate left. Rumpled and powdered with a thin coating of fine dust, both men looked as though they hadn't slept in days. Worse, the faintly lingering aroma of oozing death hovered over the duo like a dissipated cloud of polecat spray.

A second or so ticked off before Bugg pushed his grimy black Stetson to the back of a sweaty head, peered up at Longarm like he'd just found a gob of cow shit on his boot. Picked at a callus on one knuckle, then said, "Well, you star-totin' fuckers are prowlin' around mighty early in the day. What's up?"

Longarm knifed a quick glance at Fast Eddie. Gunman slumped in his chair, elbows propped against the butts of his weapons. Picked at rotting teeth with a splinter of wood. Although menacing and dangerous in the extreme, Bloodsworth appeared completely relaxed and unconcerned.

"Just wonderin' if you either of you boys happened to run across any of the Tyler bunch last night," Longarm said.

Bugg scratched an unshaven chin a bit, squirmed in his chair, then nodded. "Seems like we did get casually acquainted with one a them boys kinda late into the evenin' yestiddy. Big, ugly son of a bitch as I recall. Think his name mighta been Wade. Yeah, most assuredly coulda been. Face like a saddle-sized mound a hammered manure, ain't that right, Eddie?"

"Yeah. Mountainous, ugly son of a bitch. Pert sure he said his name was Wade. Or maybe it were Dade. Er Cade. Cain't really say, bein' as how we didn't do no more'n exchange a few pleasantries with the man."

Hamp Forbes jumped in and said, "Absolutely certain that's all you boys did? *Exchange a few pleasantries* when you met?"

Jennings flashed an impudent, toothy grin. "Long night last night. Truth be told, we haven't even been to bed as yet.

Been goin' full bore ever since we left your office yesterday afternoon. Catchin' up on our drinkin' and such. Did have to leave for a spell and stroll around town a bit. Walkin' off the liquor, don't you know. Sure you fellers understand. But, to better answer your question, as I remember last night, yeah, guess you could say that's all our meeting with Tyler amounted to, Marshal Forbes," Jennings Bugg said.

"I've had a number of reports from reputable citizens that you boys spent several hours yesterday afternoon snooping around, asking all kinds of questions about the Tyler clan."

Fast Eddie slipped a hand to the yellowed grip of one of his pistols. Tapped it with a nervous finger. "That a fact, Marshal? Ain't nothin' more'n hearsay far as I'm concerned. But while such a anonymous testimony might have a granule of truth to it, what the hell business is it of anybody's but ours who we associate with, Marshal? We ain't done nothin' wrong."

A wicked grin etched its way across Longarm's lips when he locked eyes with Jennings Bugg again. "Someone opened your recently lynched brother's grave last night, Jennings. Given that you'd already apprised us of your intention to do that selfsame thing, we just wondered if you might have carried through on your objective."

Bugg picked at a penny-sized scab on one of his knuckles. "Even if we were the ones what committed such a despicable, gruesome act as diggin' up the foully lynched corpse of my poor, pitiful, murdered brother, feel pretty sure you're gonna have a tough time provin' it, Marshal Long."

Forbes placed a foot on the seat of an empty chair from the table next to the one occupied by Bugg and Bloodsworth. Leaned an elbow onto his knee. Laid the ten-gauge blaster in the crook of his arm pointed at Jennings Bugg's stomach.

"You boys find what you were looking for, Jennings?" Forbes said.

"Where the hell's all this goin'?" Bloodsworth shot back.

"Well, seems to us that whoever unearthed your brother—which we think was probably you boys—went and filled up most of the hole with poor, ole Wade Tyler's bullet-riddled corpse," Longarm said.

A look of feigned, wide-eyed horror sprinted across Jennings Bugg's twisted countenance. "Why, that's just by God horrible. You mean to say that Tyler feller, fine gent we met and shared a beaker of spirits with just last night, has met with a foul and unfortunate end? Just curls my toenails to think of such an ill-fated happenstance."

"Damn near shot to pieces, near as we could tell from a very cursory examination at the corpse," Hamp Forbes said. "Counted five holes in his chest myself. 'Course, there might've been more I just didn't see."

Bloodsworth squinted up at Longarm. In a voice that dripped insolence, he snarled, "You star-totin' sons a bitches gonna accuse me and Jennings of somethin'? Or do you just figure on standin' here and talkin' us to death?"

Longarm locked blood-soaked gazes with Fast Eddie. Before he could answer the arrogant gunman's smart-assed question, a rumbling, stormlike roar, along with the vibration of the saloon's floorboards, announced the arrival of a sizable party of riders as they thundered in from Val Verde's west end. Clatter of iron-shod hooves on the thoroughfare's sandstone paving blocks caused such a din of racket, Hamp Forbes threw a knowing nod in Longarm's direction, then strode to the Big River's massive front window and watched as the riders passed.

Once the ruckus had died down a bit, Forbes eased back to his original spot near Jennings Bugg's corner table. A self-satisfied, toothy grin embellished his handsome face.

"What the hell you smirkin' 'bout, Forbes?" Bloodsworth snapped.

Forbes flicked Longarm a sidewise glance, then said, "Don't think we'll have to 'accuse' you boys of anything to see some eventual justice done, Eddie. Tyler bunch just rode into town. Headed over to Dobson's to pick up their brother's corpse, I'd wager."

"Do tell."

"Yeah, Bugg, that I do. See, we sent word to the remaining family earlier that we'd found Wade's butchered body."

"Why the hell should we give a shit what you said, or who rode into your pissant little village?" Jennings Bugg snapped.

Longarm chuckled, then said, "'Cause, you ignorant, big-headed wretch, once Jack Tyler, Drew, and that hell-on-wheels sister of theirs get wind that you boys, more'n anyone else in town, appear to figure in on Wade's unexpected passing, we won't have to accuse or arrest either of you. Figure both you polecats will be deader'n Santa Anna by this time tomorrow. Yep, you fellers ain't nothin' more'n dead men walkin'."

Surprised both Longarm and Forbes when Bloodsworth sharpened his gaze at them, then flashed a pleasant smile. "You law pushers actually think it bothers either of us a single whit if the Tyler bunch is in town? Or that they'll probably be scoutin' around for trouble in a bit?"

Quizzical, slightly confused looks spread across the faces of Forbes and Longarm.

"Truth is, me'n Eddie are just happier'n a couple of fat gophers in soft dirt. Hope the whole sunuvabitchin' bunch marches over here right fuckin' quicklike." He patted the butt of one of his pistols. "We've got a little somethin' waitin' for the folks that we know for damned sure took part in Charlie's illegal execution."

Longarm flicked Hamp Forbes a surprised glance, then

said, "Well, if that's the case, think we'll stick around for a spell. See exactly what you're capable of, Eddie. Maybe have an icy cold beer and wait for the show to start. How 'bout you, Marshal Forbes?"

Forbes let out a strange, uneasy, almost giggling snicker. "Absolutely. Let's take a spot yonder at the end of the bar. Throw a few glasses of cold beer back. Wait and see what happens."

Before he turned for the bar, Longarm added, "Know this, Jennings. We got caught up short when the town took Charlie. I won't stand by for a massacre today. You two go to shootin' people, and we'll have to step in. Bet the ranch you won't like the consequences."

Bugg leaned back in his chair and smiled.

A prickling sensation ran up Longarm's spine from the waist of his pants to his hairline. The prospect of imminent bloodshed seemed a foregone conclusion.

Chapter 14

Custis Long brought a sweating, icy beer mug to eager lips. Took a healthy, slurping gulp of the chilled, amber-colored liquid. Then, with what amounted to elaborate counterfeit ceremony, lowered the beaker onto its damp-circled resting spot atop the bar. Eased out his Ingersoll watch, glanced at the big ticker, then shoved it back into his vest pocket. The wary deputy U.S. marshal turned ever so slightly in Hamp Forbes's direction.

Under his breath, Longarm hissed, "This dance oughta be gettin' cranked up right soonlike, Hamp. Near as I can figure, the Tyler bunch's been over yonder at Dobson's undertakin' and buryin' operation a-ganderin' at ole Wade's corpse for nigh on forty-five minutes."

Forbes leaned against the bar on his elbows. Twirled his drink around in the sweaty wet spot atop the glistening marble beneath it. For several seconds, he stared absentmindedly into the half-empty mug of froth-covered liquid. "Well," he said as though instructing a small child, "they are a close-knit bunch, Marshal Long. Most likely, you're right. Appears they've been looking the corpse over pretty close. Be willing to bet the ranch they're talking the situation over right now."

"Reckon they've already found out about Jennings and Bloodsworth?"

"Damned good chance one of the Tyler clan's local running buddies told them about Jennings Bugg and his crew within a few minutes after their arrival in town. Now they're just trying to decide on exactly what course of action they should take. You know, like whether to kill all of us or not."

"If their actions the day they helped lynch Charlie Bugg are any indicator, I could just about guess what's next without puttin' any real serious strain on my rusted-up thinker mechanism."

Forbes shook his head. "Given your brief past experiences with the Tyler family, Long, doubt you'd think it but, truth is, the tribe's generally a right cautious bunch. Especially when it comes to important decisions that might well affect the entire crew—or get some of them killed. Tell the Gospel truth, I still find it something of a surprising abnormality that those boys lost their heads and led the assault on my jail."

"No way to justify what the bunch of lame-brained churnheads did, Hamp. In spite of the fact that ole Charlie, according to them as witnessed the foul deed, did murder the hell outta their brother."

Forbes shook his head, then nodded as though deeply saddened by the truth of the situation. "Yeah. You're absolutely right about that. From now on, we'll always have that particular piece of gnarly, factual information getting in the way of making excuses for them."

A violent rush of noise from the street rolled under the Big River Saloon's batwing doors like rumbling waves crashing against a swift-moving river's banks. The sound of booted, spurred feet clomping across the main thoroughfare's sandstone pavers snapped Longarm into erect alertness.

Empty shot glass in one hand, damp towel in the other, the Big River's daytime drink slinger, Gardner Armstrong, stumbled backward from his favored serving spot—

centermost of the bar. Wide-eyed and red-faced, he backed into the corner nearest Longarm. The bar dog sweated bullets the size of a grown man's thumb. Had the worried, strangled appearance of someone about to fall down dead from the effects of a massive stroke brought on by abject terror.

Over one shoulder, without taking his horror-stricken gaze off the cow-country oasis's front entrance, the whiskey wrangler barely breathed, "'S them Tyler boys and their belligerent sister, Marshals. Been servin' folks 'round these parts long enough that I recognize damn nigh every man's individual tread. Ain't nobody else comes 'cross the street or down the boardwalk with such confidence, authority, and downright brazen arrogance. Whole bunch of 'em's mighty damn full of themselves."

Longarm leaned on one elbow and flipped the tail of his suit coat aside. Slid a hand around the yellowed-ivory grip of the double-action Colt Lightning lying across his belly. Pulled and cocked the weapon, then held it next to his leg. Anyone approaching the cagey lawdog with evil intent would have found it difficult to determine that he already had the jump on them.

Longarm heard, but didn't see, the hammers of Hamp Forbes's shotgun snap back. Sounded like a man breaking walnuts in his fist. At that exact instant, Jack Tyler slapped the Big River's batwings aside and stepped across the liquor locker's rugged threshold. Drew and Billie Tyler stole in behind their brother, then stationed themselves on either side of him. Three men Longarm didn't recognize followed, dressed in leather chaps, stacked-heel boots, heavy cotton shirts, and the other garb typical of working cowboys. Longarm took the extra gunhands to be riders for the Tyler family's Twisted T brand. Ghostly cloud of fine, powdery dust drifted beneath the doors on a hot breeze, and quickly enveloped the entire party all the way up to their knees.

"Looks like Jack brought some help along," Longarm whispered.

"Guess he figured he might need someone covering his back," Forbes said.

Several seconds of deathly quiet crawled past as the surly party's darting, ratlike eyes adjusted to the more subdued daytime illumination inside the bar's dimly lit interior. Jack Tyler cast a fleeting glance at Longarm and Hamp Forbes, but acted as though he'd not seen either man. Then, of a sudden, Tyler jerked his chin around, and the entire group moved toward Jennings Bugg's corner table as though all six functioned as a single entity.

Longarm and Marshal Forbes swiveled tense gazes to follow the party's movement. Watched as the Tyler crew drew up but a few steps from Jennings Bugg's table.

Appeared to have surprised the surly group more than a bit when a sneering, steely-eyed Eddie Bloodsworth uncoiled and slid out of his chair like a desert sidewinder on the prowl amongst rabbits. Gunfighter backed up against the wall, behind and a bit to Jennings Bugg's left. Bloodsworth's rock-steady hands hovered above the grips of glittering pistol butts.

Bugg, who had at some point pulled his chair so far up under the felt-covered poker table his paws couldn't be seen, stared into the bottom of a half-filled whiskey glass. Without bothering to look up, he said, "Well, well, well. Do somethin' for you gents—and the lady?"

Jack Tyler exploded. He shook a knotted finger Bugg's direction. "We just spent nigh on an hour starin' into the bloodless face of my dead brother, mister. Undertaker tells me as how, near as he's able to tell, somebody went'n shot 'im eight times. Five in front, three in back."

Calm as the surface of a cattle tank on a windless day, Bugg didn't appear to move or react. Sounded as though speaking from the bottom of a well when he said, "Do tell.

'S damned tragic. Yessir, damned tragic. 'Pears as how a man ain't safe nowheres these days."

Drew Tyler, who'd not spoken a single word, made a clumsy grab for the gun strapped high on his waist, but Jack grabbed his brother's wrist. Near the top of his lungs, a struggling Drew Tyler yelled, "Hear tell you two're probably the ones what done fer Wade. Ain't a soul 'round here'd have guts enough to commit such an act, and ain't no other strangers around town but you bastards."

The sudden movement and yelling sent the tension in the Big River's main room shooting through the roof. Twitchy cowboys watching the Tyler clan's backs nervously glanced around the room. Pinch-browed and gritting their teeth, all three looked worried, confused, and more than a little unsettled. Just not used to this kind of confrontation, Longarm thought to himself.

Bloodsworth brought his head back and flicked death-dealing glances at each of the Tyler crew. Man looked down his nose, as though staring into a box full of Mexican cockroaches. Thin, cruel, top lip curled away from tobacco-stained teeth when he said, "We don't know nothin' 'bout your dead relative, mister. 'Cept maybe what the town marshal just got done a-tellin' us."

Billie Tyler slapped her ubiquitous riding crop against one leather-sheathed leg and barked, "You're a lyin' son of a bitch, mister. And on top a that, you're uglier'n a mud fence decorated with a ton of cow shit."

Bloodsworth's stubble-covered, pox-scarred face went white. Man tensed up like a knotted plow line. "Nobody calls me a liar. 'N I do mean nobody. Not even a mean-mouthed bitch like you."

Using his off arm and hand, Jack Tyler continued to wrestle with his struggling, red-faced brother. Drew, the taller and heavier of the pair, craned his neck over Jack's shoulder and yelped, "No man livin' calls my sister a bitch, mister. Unbuckle them pistol belts, you mouthy cocksucker. I'll kick yer ass till yer nose bleeds like somebody went 'n cut yer fuckin' head off with an ax."

As though speaking to a group of misbehaving children, Jennings Bugg grinned, then said, "Way I heard it, ain't no doubt a'tall that you boys, you Tylers that is, are solely responsible for the lynchin' of my brother, Charlie."

Billie shook her quirt in Jennings Bugg's face. "The stupid bastard murdered Buster."

Bugg hit his feet so quick the table almost tipped over as it bounced forward two feet. His chair ricocheted off the wall. Both of the angry killer's hands came up filled with cocked pistols. Before the Tylers or any of their riders could even think about blinking twice, Fast Eddie Bloodsworth had them covered as well.

Purple-faced and slavering, Bugg roared, "Then he shoulda hung, you silly, hate-filled bitch. Legal-like. Shoulda been a trial. In a court. With a judge, jury, and lawyers to see to all the niceties. And if found guilty, he shoulda gone to the gallows. But not like some kinda crazed animal dragged from its cage by a bunch of bloodthirsty, small-town avengers carryin' a piece of twisted hemp."

Hamp Forbes's voice shook when he whispered, "Long, you reckon we should step up and put an end to this before somebody gets shot graveyard dead?"

Longarm, with the prickling sensations of imminent gunfire and certain death still washing up and down his spine, tilted his head toward Val Verde's marshal. Forbes barely heard him when Longarm hissed, "We could. Might get us killed as well, though. May be best to just let 'em go at it, Hamp. See to them as are left standin'."

"Jesus, we could have a massacre of Biblical porportions if we don't do something," Forbes hissed back.

Jack Tyler struggled as he held his brother's arm in one hand, his sister's in the other. Tyler's three backup riders, jumpy, frightened, and confused by the unexpected turn of circumstances, appeared paralyzed. All three cast nervous glances that flitted around the room as though searching for the nearest convenient exit.

Struggling to keep a grip on his angry siblings, Tyler said, "'Fore we come over here from Dobson's undertakin' operation, Bugg, my brother, sister, and I talked all this over. Decided as how we didn't want to sully Wade's memory with another killin' this soon after his sorry passin'."

Jennings Bugg sneered. "Given the position you now find yourself in, Tyler, I could care fuckin' less than a steamin' pile of runny manure about your murderous family's feelings of bullshit benevolence. Now, I think you insolent bastards and the crazy bitch you brought with you had best get on outta my sight, and damned quick. Go on and bury your dead. Make an effort to deal with your grief."

Near Big River's entrance a voice called out, "I second that motion. Think you'd best take the man's advice."

From the corner of one eye, Longarm spotted Bathsheba Bugg, short-barreled shotgun in hand, standing at the opposite end of the bar. The fiery-eyed girl's inexplicable entrance proved something of a mystery for the Denver-based lawdog. Normally, he wouldn't have missed such a danger-tinged occurrence.

Longarm nudged Hamp Forbes. "Now's the time. Shoulder that big popper of yours. Cover my back. Let me do the talkin'."

Forbes's lips trembled when he said, "Works for me," then stepped aside to let the deputy U.S. marshal out front of the pair.

Almost everyone in the room flinched in genuine surprise when Longarm thundered, "All right, that's enough. Think you and Bloodsworth best put those weapons aside, Jennings. Either of you go and pull the trigger on any of these men right now, and I'll blast you out of your boots."

Bugg sighted along the barrel of the pistol he'd made an ever so slight move at pointing in Longarm's direction.

"You bring that shooter to bear on me, you'd best be ready to use it, Jennings," Longarm roared. "Ain't messin' with a bunch of West Texas brush poppers when you pull down on the federal law."

Bugg's cocked weapon froze in place. He whispered something to Bloodsworth; then both men slowly holstered their weapons.

"Time you Tyler boys packed it in, headed on back to the Twisted T, and saw to Wade's services," Longarm said. "Sure you've probably got a family plot out on the ranch where you can lay him to rest."

Jack Tyler swung his fevered gaze toward Longarm and Hamp Forbes. He let a transitory glance dart from one of their firearm's open muzzles to the next, seemed to discount their presence, and then carefully eyeballed the rest of the room. Tyler's scathing gaze stopped on Bathsheba Bugg. Unlike her brother, she had not given an inch. Her cocked shotgun was leveled at Jack's head.

"Looks like you've got us," Tyler said. "Wouldn't be much of a contest if'n we were to go grabbin' for our smoke wagons, now would it?"

"None," Longarm agreed. "Glad you've seen the light, Jack. Nothin' like a little religion and a couple of fully primed shotguns to help a man get closer to God."

Jack Tyler gritted his teeth so loud, Longarm heard it all the way across the room.

"Now, here's the way I see this dance workin'," Longarm said. "Want all you fellers nearest me and Marshal Forbes to slowly turn around, one at a time, and head for the door. Once all of you're out in the street, best get on back to Dobson's, pick up Wade's body. Then get yourselves mounted and head on out of town."

Jack threw a curt nod toward the batwings and, as instructed, the Tyler party moved for the door in a nervous, red-faced, defeated line. A fuming Drew Tyler and all the other cowboys made it outside with no further problems. Damned near purple around the gills, Billie Tyler evidently had something else in mind.

Only woman in the Tyler bunch drew to a stop no more than five or six steps in front of Bathsheba Bugg. Leveled her silver-headed quirt at Jennings's grinning sister and said, "Next time you point a gun at me, you crazy bitch, best be usin' it."

"Oh, God," Hamp Forbes said, "the bitch word again. If these women don't kill each other, we'll be blessed in ways I'll have to thank God for tonight, Long."

"Just keep on walkin'," Bathsheba growled.

Hesitating with every step, Billie held the abbreviated whip in front of her. Almost bent it double between gloved hands as she continued the slow journey to the Big River's still-swinging batwings. She kept a hot-eyed gaze locked on Bathsheba Bugg. Her aggressive demeanor and behavior did not change one whit when she stood in the doorway and said, "Don't be lettin' me or any of our men catch you outside town. Any of you. Trust me. You'll damn sure regret it."

When the mouthy gal finally turned and left nothing behind but the flopping saloon doors and a drifting cloud of dust, Bathsheba Bugg lowered the hammers on her shotgun but kept it trained on the exit and at the ready.

A humor-tinged smile played across the Bugg woman's face when she said, "Right sassy little thing, ain't she."

Soon as everyone but Jack was waiting outside on the boardwalk, he turned, pointed a finger at Jennings Bugg again, and said, "Best get yourself ready for it, mister. Your time on this earth is just about over. Right now, I'm gonna see that all my family gets back home for the funeral. We'll observe one day of mourning. Then I'm comin' back to kill you. You wanna stay alive, Bugg, best light a shuck and get the hell outta Val Verde."

He started for the Big River's entrance again, but stopped with one hand resting atop the swinging doors. Turned back toward the watchful marshals and said, "Warnin' you in no uncertain terms, Hamp. You lawdogs best stay outta the way on this one. Us Tylers don't have any real desire to kill a lawman, but in this instance, I'll sure 's hell make an exception. Aim to kill these two sons a bitches in just about two days from now. You hear me, Hamp?"

Forbes nodded but didn't reply.

"No rawhidin' here. I'll say it one more time just to be clearer'n a glass of rainwater. Both of you'd better keep the hell outta this." And with that, he pushed through the batwings and disappeared onto the street.

As he holstered his own weapon, Longarm waved in Bathsheba Bugg's direction and said, "Put that damned thing away."

Oozing an air of cheeky insolence, Jennings Bugg's sister laid her big blaster across one arm and strode to a spot at the bar only a few feet from where Longarm stood. Like a sex-starved alley cat, she eyeballed the stringy-muscled lawdog from his boot soles to the crown of his Stetson. Once again, her brazen ogling lingered on his crotch way longer than propriety would have dictated.

"Well, by God, that was right invigoratin'," Bathsheba said, and continued to shamelessly stare at Longarm from beneath her hat brim. "Come damn nigh dryin' my throat up like a two-hundred-mile stretch of the Sierra del Huacha Mountains," she added. "How 'bout buyin' me a drink, Marshal Long? Sure could use a jolt of somethin' to kinda *take the edge off*."

Longarm flicked a finger in drink wrangler Gardner Armstrong's direction. Then he pointed to a spot on the bar near Bathsheba Bugg's elbow. And though mildly distracted by a missing button on the feisty gal's shirt that exposed a goodly portion of a heavy-nippled breast, he kept a tense, wary look locked on Jennings and Fast Eddie Bloodsworth.

Amidst extensive noise and to-do, the grinning gal's brother and their lethal compadre set to dragging their table back into its original position. Worked like a couple of old crones at reclaiming what looked to be turning into their favored corner spot located smack in the middle of the Tyler family's pet drinking establishment.

After considerable pointing, rearranging, and shuffling, a bit of halfhearted grousing and general fooling around, Bugg and Bloodsworth finally got things just the way they wanted them, then flopped back into their chairs. Pair appeared more than a bit satisfied as they ordered up a fresh bottle of Old Skull Popper and set to work on a course that appeared designed to make sure they drank themselves into an unmoving stupor—and as quickly as humanly possible.

In spite of efforts to the contrary, Longarm couldn't help but also take notice of the hungry-eyed Bathsheba's wet-lipped, appreciative gaze. When he thought the girl wasn't strictly paying attention, he snatched a number of guarded glances in her direction. Gal persisted with her obsessive eyeballing. Grabbed up the double shot of rye Gardner Armstrong slid to her from the middle of the bar. Then, with no more than a second's glance at the glass, threw the liquor back like a hundred-year-old, burnt-dry desert rat that had stopped by for its first mouthful of coffin paint in a decade.

Longarm pitched coins onto the bar. Money bounced and jingled. "Let's go, Hamp," he said. "Our work here is done—for the immediate time being at any rate. Think we can keep a better eye on the street from the porch out front of your office."

As he tried to move past Bathsheba Bugg, Longarm got half a step closer than he had intended. One of the girl's hands snaked between them and surreptitiously caressed his bulging crotch.

"My, oh, my, but you are one strong, healthy, good-lookin' man," Bathsheba grunted, and gave his dingus an affectionate squeeze. "No need to hurry off," she added when he failed to stop. "Why don't you stick around, handsome. Hell's bells, real fun ain't even got started yet. All this you seen so far ain't nothin' but a lead-in to bigger'n better things, Marshal Long."

Longarm could still hear the girl's tinkling, musical laughter following along behind when he stepped onto the boardwalk out front of the marshal's office on the far side of the street.

Hamp Forbes propped his still-loaded shotgun against the door frame of the office. Jerked a bandanna from a hip pocket and ran it beneath a dripping chin. "Whew. Boy oh howdy, it's a hot one."

"Yes it is," Longarm said between teeth clenched around the end of the nickel cheroot he worked at lighting.

"Don't know about you, Marshal Long, but I'm damned glad our little dance with Jack Tyler and Jennings Bugg didn't develop into a shooting match."

Longarm leaned against a porch pillar and blew smoke skyward. "Right there with you, Hamp. Have to admit as how shootin' people just ain't near as much fun as it used to be."

"Longer I manage to stay alive, and the more years I put on, the less inclined I am to trade lead with really bad men who aren't standing much more than a dozen feet from me. Too damned dangerous, you ask me."

"Sure enough pays to stay wary when it comes to men like Bugg and Bloodsworth." Longarm said. "Sometimes appears that everything men like them boys lay a hand on turns to rigor mortis faster'n the average man can blow out a lamp."

Forbes gave a dispirited shake of the head, then snatched the big shooter-up. As he stepped across the threshold and into his office, he said, "I'm not getting paid enough for this kind of botheration. Think I'll sit me down and give some thought to the possibility of afterlife redemption for a few minutes."

"Sounds like a plan, Hamp. Best go on and do 'er. I'll lounge around out here. Watch the street for you till it gets dark. Don't think we'll have much of nothin' to worry ourselves about from them Tylers. Leastways, not till they try and make good on Jack's threat."

Forbes grunted and disappeared inside the jailhouse.

Longarm snuggled up against his porch pillar and took a deep drag on his stogie. Across the street, he could see Bathsheba Bugg peeking at him over the Big River Saloon's batwing doors.

Chapter 15

Longarm flicked the gooey stub of a smoldering nickel cheroot into Val Verde's stone-covered street. He stared down the length of the main thoroughfare, past all the houses and buildings. Gazed into the vast, quickly darkening, empty stretches of sand and mesquite beyond the town's sharply demarcated limits. A sickle-shaped slice of sun the color of molten iron sizzled its way to a spot somewhere beneath the western horizon. Heaven's smoldering orb was headed for darkness like a burning, four-masted warship on its way to the bottom of the ocean.

Out of habit more than anything else, the now-relaxed lawman resettled his pistol belt. Made sure the hammer loop on his holster was pushed aside and out of the way. Lifted the Colt Lightning, then loosely slipped it back into place, in an effort to make sure there would be no problem should he need quick access.

He did one more squint-eyed check of everything he could see along the boardwalks. The street, now lit by a string of flickering lamps atop metal poles, held barely half a dozen or so citizens out for an evening's stroll. Appeared most of the walkers had gravitated to those shallow, ragged pools of yellow-tinted light nearest the entrances of the Rio Grande Saloon, the Bishop Hotel, Crabb's Big River, Bob's Café, and a barbershop next to the telegraph office. Movement around the front gate to Bell's Livery, Stable, and Corral proved hard to discern, as no streetlight was located anywhere nearby.

Appeared to Longarm that the Tylers had made good on their word. Nothing else out of the way had occurred for more than two hours, and none of the justifiably belligerent bunch had returned with blood flashing in their eyes. Thank God. Jennings Bugg, his sister Bathsheba, and their deadly friend Fast Eddie Bloodsworth continued to celebrate the way they had so easily buffaloed the Tylers at the Big River Saloon. A quick glance over Longarm's shoulder, through the jailhouse's barred window, revealed a napping Hamp Forbes. Chin on chest, bootless feet propped in a drawer of his desk, Val Verde's resident lawman snored like a crosscut saw ripping through hundred-year-old oak.

Pleased with the town's seemingly tranquil disposition, Longarm stoked another rum-soaked cheroot to life. Flipped the dead match into the street, then headed for his room in Doc Hughes's infirmary.

Came as something of a surprise when, expecting an evening's tussle before turning in for the night, Longarm ambled into the clinic and discovered that the more-than-willing Nettie was nowhere to be found. Way he figured it, she must have gone with her father on one of his out-of-town calls.

On his way down the clinic's front-to-back hallway, the disappointed and suddenly bone-weary deputy U.S. marshal took time to turn off each of the four coal oil lamps hanging every few feet along the wall. Quick as the door of his room clicked shut, he stripped, then stretched out naked atop the crisp starched and ironed bedsheets.

Longarm hadn't realized how really tired he was until his heavy head hit the pillow. Open window, near the foot of the bed, let in a cool, relaxing, wildflower-scented evening breeze. Within a matter of minutes, Deputy U.S. Marshal Custis Long slept like the proverbial dead man.

Nettie Hughes popped up in the second, or maybe third, dream Longarm had that night. Even though steeped in a state of profoundly deep slumber, he unconsciously found the realistic quality of the lifelike vision downright unsettling. Got jerked about in his sleep several times, as though shocked by the randy girl's freely given libidinous gifts. Seemed almost as though he could actually feel the energetic Nettie's gushing cooz, as it engulfed his rigid prong in silken heat and, with lively zeal, sucked back and forth along the sensitive shaft. The dreamy sensation became so intense, he snapped upright in the bed and blinked open sleep-heavy eyes.

Bathed in the soft, silvery glow of moonlight that poured beneath the paper window shade and oozed into the room, a buck-assed naked Bathsheba Bugg sat on the edge of the bed beside him. One hand was buried in her own crotch—up to the wrist. With a gentleness that belied all her previously observable behavior, she ran the tantalizing, tickling fingers of the other hand up and down Longarm's thick, turgid prong. At the same time, she nibbled, kissed, sucked, and flicked an incredibly long, snaky tongue around the massive, fleshy, sensitive tip.

"Sweet Jesus, girl. How'd you get in here?" Longarm grunted.

With the head of his cock lodged against her cheek, she let out a hoarse, whiskey-laced chuckle, then said, "Window. Come through the window. How else?"

"Well, it's a damned good thing I didn't wake up and go to grabbin' for iron while you were doin' that. Mighta shot hell outta you."

"Well, if'n you'z gonna shoot me, I'd much prefer you did it 'fore I done went and got all my duds off. Might look kinda bad if'n you kilt me now and Marshal Forbes was forced to investigate the shootin'. Found me a-layin' 'side the bed suckin' on my own nipple. Both hands 'tween my legs. 'Sides, shoot me now and you'll miss out on the best blow job of your entire lifetime. I've got a tongue that'll put a shine on your knob the likes of what you've never experienced, Bubba."

"Well, I don't know 'bout tha—"

Bathsheba's steamy, slobbery mouth opened as she leaned forward. Hungry, wet lips slid over the reddened, bulbous head of his rampant love muscle. Sucking all the way, she surprised Longarm by getting near half his enormous pecker into her ravenous mouth and down a waiting throat. Giving himself over to the overwhelming sensation the gifted girl evoked, he leaned back into his pillow, placed both hands behind his head, and relaxed.

Fingers comfortably laced together, Longarm watched as Bathsheba's talented, puffing cheeks expanded and contracted. No doubt about it, the pocket-sized gal had an astonishing ability to tongue, suck, lick, and chew on his raging whanger all at the same time. Perhaps even more amazing, she energetically accomplished all her astonishing tricks while more than half his fleshy tool was lodged against the back of her throat.

Bathsheba's full, slurping lips slid the length of his dong. She flicked her tongue against the underside of the head, then stabbed at its slitlike eye with the pointed, snaky tip. She sucked the head back into her mouth and lodged it just behind her teeth. The distinct, overwhelming sensations brought on by the twirling movements of the gifted muscle in the girl's clever mouth jerked Longarm to a sitting position as though he'd been struck with the popper of a well-applied bullwhip.

He grasped Bathsheba by the shoulders, flipped her onto the bed, and jerked her beneath him. To his surprise, the woman fought, scratched, clawed, and bit like something wild. She giggled, squirmed, and bounced her steamy quim away when he tried to pin her to the mattress with a length of love muscle that had achieved a state of hardness similar to a town smithy's horseshoe tongs. Appeared as though the playful gal enjoyed the wrestling match as much as, or more than, the inevitable screwing that awaited if she would've stopped squirming around.

Finally forced to decisive action, Longarm grabbed Bathsheba by the throat. He pushed the scrappy, giggling girl into the pillow. Forced her legs apart with one knee, then plowed into the furry muff of sopping wet heat at the juncture of flailing thighs.

Both Bathsheba's sharp-clawed hands sliced their way down his back, then clamped onto his flint-hard butt cheeks. A high-pitched, chirping squeal that could have shattered glass escaped her trembling lips as Longarm finally hit the bottom of her. Fingers clamped over the yelping gal's open mouth dramatically cut the lusty racket as he pounded his stiff love muscle into slick, gushing, fluttering flesh.

Thirty or so minutes into the ride, the feisty gal somehow managed to wrestle her way to a spot astride Longarm's narrow waist. Hands lodged against his chest, she leaned her weight slightly forward. Bounced up and down on his unyielding prong like an escapee from an insane asylum straddling a crazed bronc. In a matter of seconds, she had worked herself into a frothy-crotched frenzy unlike any in Longarm's vast carnal experience.

Bathsheba's riotous bucking and snorting continued for an uncommonly long time. Amused by the girl's energetic lovemaking, Longarm occasionally snatched bored glances at the Ingersoll watch atop his bedside table. Barely able to make out the timepiece's hands in the silvery moonlight, he watched in amazement as nigh on an hour ticked off before the energetic gal finally appeared to wilt a bit.

"Yes. Yes. Yes. Oh, fuckin' yes," she hissed into his ear. "Comin'. I'm comin'. Oh, God. Oh, God. Oh, God. Never. Never. Fuckin' ain't never felt like this. Oh, there it is again." Of a sudden, she slowed. Plopped her dripping notch down against his pubic bone, and let her entire upper body sag against him. "Shit. Think I'm gonna pass out," she said, then slowly rolled onto her side.

Longarm's unbending dingus made a loud sucking *plop* as it exited Bathsheba's dripping snatch. Slick with sweat, covered in the glistening sheen of steamy sex and other bodily fluids, he chuckled, then playfully smacked the girl's shapely, muscular caboose.

"Shouldna had . . . so much to . . . drink," Bathsheba grunted. "Wasn't so fuckin' drunk, I coulda . . . rode you . . . right into the ground, by God. Wore that big ole thang a yours down to a stubby li'l nub . . . Jus' like sharpenin' a pencil."

"Well, cain't go and give up so quick then, can we now, darlin'. Still got some whittlin' to do yet. Hell, this oughta wake you up," he said, then swung his feet to the floor and stood. Grabbed the girl up as though she weighed less than a sackful of goose down.

With Bathsheba strapped around his waist like a living belt, Longarm ambled over to the open window, then eased her shapely ass down onto the sill. "Damned sight cooler over here. Bit of a breeze," he said, then leaned through the unscreened opening and grasped the frame on either side.

Rubbery arms locked around her tireless lover's neck, a near-lifeless Bathsheba Bugg could do little more than lay back into the open air and hang on for dear life. Longarm started that particular session slowly, but in a matter of minutes his stringy-muscled, pile-driving ass had his steely tool smacking into her gushing flesh like the pushrod on a Baldwin engine being stoked to maximum steam pressure.

In the glow of moonlight that bathed Bathsheba's sweat-drenched face, Longarm watched as her eyes rolled into the back of her head. When it appeared the girl had gone totally limp, he snatched her off the windowsill. Flopped down onto a chair next to the door with her spread-eagle atop him once again.

He kept the gushing action going by grasping Bathsheba

around the waist and resuming the lively, bucking ride she'd enjoyed earlier in the evening. When, after another thirty minutes or so, the ashen-faced girl collapsed against his chest, Longarm stood, dropped her onto the bed, and flipped her onto her tawny, table-flat belly. Standing beside the bed, he grabbed her hips, lifted her off the mattress, shoved his rampant cock into her waiting flesh again, and pumped until he was so tired, he rolled onto one side and drifted off to sleep.

Early the following morning, Longarm drifted in and out of sleep. An irritating banging somewhere inside his head refused to go away. Groggy and muddle-brained, he wallowed his way to a sitting position against the bed's iron-doweled headboard. Squinting against the leaden glare of daybreak knifing its way through his room's only window, he pawed amongst the sheets in a halfhearted attempt to find his partner from the previous evening's romp. Bathsheba Bugg appeared to have vanished in much the same way she had appeared. No physical indication of the girl's late-night visit remained. However, the lingering aroma of sex still hovered over the bed.

A series of sharp raps on the door jarred the bleary-eyed lawman into something nigh on to awareness. He eyeballed the portal, then said, "Yeah. Who is it?"

Hamp Forbes pushed his way into the room. Immediately headed for the window and forced it open as far as it would go. "Christ, Long, smells like somebody's been breeding pigs in here."

Covered with nothing but a rumpled, sweat-drenched sheet, Longarm snatched a nickel cheroot from atop the nightstand and fired it to smoldering life. A deep, satisfying drag on the stogie appeared to revive him. "Not sure the wondrously talented Miss Bathsheba Bugg would like being compared to a pig, Marshal Forbes—even one that could dance. Fact is, I'm pretty damned certain the lady'd be downright insulted. Hot-assed little gal just might jerk a knot in your arrogant ass for sayin' such a thing."

"Sweet Jesus," Forbes said. "Should have figured on something like this after the way she acted yesterday over at the Big River. In spite of the somewhat tense nature of our encounter, could tell the girl had developed something of a serious itch when it came to you, Long."

Longarm grinned, took a jaunty puff from his cigar, then said, "Well, Marshal Forbes, way I figure it, scrappy little gal got scratched pretty good last night, even if I do say so myself. Yessir, figure the randy-assed Miss Bugg won't be needing another scratchin' for some time to come."

Forbes fanned the air with his hat. "Best get on up, Long. We've got something of a *situation* we've gotta look into."

Custis Long rubbed one temple as though trying to massage away a piercing headache. "What kind of 'situation' might that be, Marshal?"

Forbes stomped across the room. Stopped in the open doorway. Fidgeted with his hat. Then, over his shoulder, said, "You can get a quick bath across the street at Jookie Taylor's Barber Shop, Marshal Long. And trust me, way you smell, you need a good scrubbing. Think you'd best get moving right this minute. I'll meet you out front of Jookie's in exactly thirty minutes. Have your animal saddled and ready for you. Ain't much of a ride. Mite less than a mile. But I don't care to walk it in the kind of heat we're going to have in about an hour or so."

Smoldering cigar clenched between his teeth, Longarm said, "What the hell's goin' on, Hamp?"

Forbes shook his head. "Not altogether certain myself, Custis. Rancher named Ernie Blocker, who has a small horse-raising operation out west of town, just came by my office and said there was something out on the edge of town I probably needed to see. All I can say right now is that, if what he described to me is true, we've got a hellacious day ahead of us."

Longarm scratched a spot on his jaw. "Well, that's got a right ominous sound to it."

Forbes muttered, "If what Ernie told me is true, do believe an already bad situation might be about to get one hell of a lot worse."

With that, Val Verde's cryptic lawdog hustled off down Doc Hughes's hallway and left Custis Long sitting atop the sheets of his rank-smelling bed with a quizzical look pasted on his haggard face.

Chapter 16

Wispy clouds of pale, gritty dust wafted up around his hay burner's feet, then drifted away like silent, angry ghosts. Shaved, bathed, and smelling of lilac, Longarm sat his foot-stamping mount and stared unbelieving at the bug-eyed, black-tongued, heat-bloated carcass. Drew Tyler's battered corpse dangled from a braided piece of hemp draped over the twisted, gnarled live oak's lowest limb. Large ebon-colored grackles skittered and danced along the same thick bough, or rode the swinging cadaver's sloped shoulders. The noisy, inquisitive birds squawked, pecked at each other, and cocked their feathered heads from side to side in an apparent effort to focus flat, beady yellow eyes on a juicy, prospective lunch.

"Looks to me like he's been swingin' for quite a spell. Probably all night. Already startin' to swell up a bit. This kinda heat, he's gonna bust right open before you know it," Longarm said, then turned to Hamp Forbes. "This the same tree where Val Verde's righteous, upright, Christian citizens strung up Charlie Bugg?"

White-faced as a fresh-washed bedsheet, Forbes fidgeted with his animal's reins, sighed, then gave a halfhearted nod. "That it is," he said, and tried not to look directly at the brutish atrocity that silently twisted back and forth above and in front of them.

Longarm stared at the back of the hand draped over his saddle's pommel. Picked at a scabbed-over scratch on one knuckle and said, "Gruesome thought, I know, but do you reckon the poor bastard was still alive when he got hoisted?"

Forbes grunted as though an unseen attacker had smacked him in the chest with a closed fist the size of a blacksmith's favorite anvil. Val Verde's marshal looked stricken when he coughed into one hand, then said, "Would certainly appear to be the case. From where I'm sitting, seems to me as how whoever pulled him up there beat the unmerciful hell out of him first, though."

"Sure 'nough looks that way, don't it?"

"Guess he might have been unconscious at the time. Damn sure hope so. Swear 'fore Jesus, Long, face all busted up that way, looks like somebody went at the big ole boy with a long-handled shovel."

"Beat on him pretty good."

"Better than good. Pounded him to a bloody pulp first, then raised him up and let him dangle. Way his tongue's poking out, all swollen and black like that, wasn't any fall to crack his neck. Must've choked to death. Sorry way to die."

Custis Long stepped off his fidgeting horse, dropped the reins, and walked a complete circle around the ghastly, misshapen hanging tree. He squatted over the disturbed earth at his feet several times, and scratched in the dust with a foot-long piece of broken twig. Stared into the distance, then shook his head in disgust.

"Well, we won't get much in the way of help tryin' to figure this mess out by lookin' 'round here, Hamp. Don't take any old-time mountain man of a trackin' genius to see as how damn near every swingin' dick in Crockett County musta rode over, or through, this exact spot during the past couple a days. Ground's been pulverized to powder for near a foot down."

"Can't say as that comes as much of a surprise to me, Marshal Long. There's still plenty of folks from all over three counties strolling by here to get a look at the infamous spot where that legendary killer Charlie Bugg went to meet his Maker at the hands of an irate, justice-seeking populace. Probably still have visitors to this very location twenty years from now."

"Wouldn't surprise me."

"Likely as not, the town fathers will have to build a tree-shaded, fenced-in park, decked out with imported shrubbery, right on this very site. Put up a marble monument with a bronze plaque attached commemorating the dreadful events that occurred here. Before we know it, there'll be hawkers all over this whole vicinity selling popped corn and ice cold root beer. Have troupes of actors playing out the various parts of those involved three times daily, a mere ten cents to watch the glorious tale unfold."

Longarm appeared not to have heard his cohort's rambling rant. "Must be fifty different sets of sign within spittin' distance of this fuckin' tree. Radiate out in every direction. Apache shaman couldn't pick a decent trail outta this mess with a divinin' rod made out of solid Mexican silver."

Forbes waved Longarm's cutting comments aside, as though dealing with a nuisance flying insect. "Hell, Long, we don't need to find a trail of any kind in the first place. We both know who did this. Leastways, there's no doubt in my mind about it."

Longarm snapped the twig, tossed it aside, and stood. "Seems to me like we've already had this conversation at least once, Hamp. Thinkin's one thing. Knowin's an altogether different animal. You've been in the law-bringin' business long enough to understand that."

"I know. I know."

"Hell, we've already seen how Bugg and Bloodsworth weaseled out of any responsibility for diggin' ole Charlie up and then killin' Wade and puttin' him in the empty grave. No witnesses for none of that either. And they sure as hell ain't gonna come cryin' to us with a heartfelt confession talkin' 'bout how they wanna get right with Jesus."

"All true. Every word. But still and all, there's not a single doubt in my mind that Jennings Bugg and Fast Eddie Bloodsworth are the hard-case parties responsible for every single thing you just described. And this particular killing as well. Be willing to bet you double my next year's pay on it. Give you two-to-one odds."

"Have no doubt you're as right as a barrelful of fresh-fallen, crystal-clear rainwater. This one's something of a puzzler, though, don't you think? I mean, don't it just set you to wonderin' how Jennings and Bloodsworth managed to catch ole Drew alone?"

"Had wondered about that myself already."

"Hell, I thought the Tyler bunch was supposed to be stayin' away from town out on their ranch. All of 'em puffy-eyed and red-nosed with sorrow over the loss of Wade. Whole bunch 'uz 'sposed to be cryin', prayin', and gettin' ready for the buryin'. How in the blue-eyed hell did Drew end up out here in the middle of the night swingin' from a tree limb?"

Hamp Forbes's face turned into a mask of noncommittal befuddlement. "Beats hell out of me. Just like ole Wade's passing, we may never know how they pulled this one off either. Tell you one thing, though, Long. Think we'd best get on back to town. Run Bugg and Bloodsworth to ground. Drag them over the coals a bit and see what they've got to say."

Longarm looked thoughtful. "Yeah. Yeah. Well, no matter what else, gotta admit one thing for certain sure."

"What's that?"

"Those ole boys sure have some right creative ways of gettin' rid of Tylers. Might be kind of interesting just to sit around on our hands and wait to see what happens to Jack and Billie. Can't say as I'd be surprised to find 'em both cooked up in a pie."

Forbes grimaced, then made a face like he'd just sucked on something sour.

Longarm clambered back onto his mount. Rivers of salt-laced sweat began to run from every open pore. The saddle creaked and popped under his sodden weight. He'd barely got settled when, of a sudden, a pained expression bubbled across his freshly shaved, pink-cheeked countenance.

"What's the problem? What are you thinking about now?" Forbes said.

Longarm scratched his chin and looked thoughtful. "You don't reckon Jennings Bugg's smart enough to send that wild-assed sister over to Doc Hughes's place to keep me busy all night long while he and Fast Eddie did this, do you?"

Val Verde's marshal reined his animal back toward town and gave the beast a gentle touch of the spur. "Nothing about either of those evil bastards would surprise me, Long. Don't have to do anything more than look in Jennings Bugg's eyes to see he's about as twisted as any sidewinder the pair of us could drag from under a rock out here in the sandy wilds. Even if we had the time to search out and find such a snake."

"You're not answerin' my question, Hamp."

"All right. All right. Here it is. Here's the answer. I personally think the snaky bastard would send his mean-mouthed, bandy-legged sister to fuck all the devil's imps if it would serve whatever evil purpose Jennings Bugg had in mind. Wouldn't surprise me to find out he used her name to lure Drew out here to his death."

"Now that's a thought."

"Yeah. Maybe they sent word to the big, stupid son of a bitch that Bathsheba was waiting for him right here under this tree, buck naked, with her hand up her snatch. And when ole Drew showed up with a pecker like a fresh-forged crowbar and thinking whatever in the hell he was thinking, Bugg or Bloodsworth hit him in the head, beat the unmerciful hell out of him, and there you have it."

Longarm feigned a look of flabbergasted surprise. "Well, bless my britches, Marshal Forbes. Glad you didn't hold anything back. Sounded like you've been needin' to get all that off your chest for some time past."

The Denver-based lawman had moved but a short distance away from the hanging tree when he twisted in his saddle and glanced back at the dead man one last time. "'S one helluva sight, ain't he."

"Think this is bad, you should've seen what was left of Charlie Bugg. That one made me sicker than a poisoned pup when we came out here to take him down."

"Damn. Well, we just gonna leave ole Drew hangin' up there like that? All puffed up and swayin' in the breeze? I mean, I 'uz just thinkin' as how maybe we might wanna do the civilized thing and cut him down. Lay his big dumb ass out on the ground till we can get back and scoop 'im up."

"No need. Went by and spoke with Hiram Dobson while you were having your shave and bath. He's supposed to send a wagon out to pick up the body later this morning."

"Ah. Well, that's good. That's good."

"Maybe. Maybe not. Soon as Hiram realizes the dead man's Drew Tyler, everyone in town will know it in a matter of minutes. Word will most assuredly get back to the remainder of the Tyler family, and I mean mighty damned quicklike. Don't matter what Jack and Billie said yesterday. Probably have a damned gang of those Twisted T boys come riding down on Val Verde looking to rip the whole town a new asshole. Figure it's about nine o'clock right now. Bet they'll be here ready to kill hell out of somebody before noon comes and goes."

The ride back to Hamp Forbes's office took less than ten minutes. As the lawmen stepped from their animals' backs, Longarm jerked his chin toward the covered boardwalk out front of the Big River Saloon. "That's Jennings and Bloodsworth sittin' on those benches down yonder, ain't it, Hamp?"

Forbes tried to look casual. He fiddled with his saddle's cinch strap. Stared over the animal's back and said, "Yes indeed. That's them, all right. You want to stroll on over and brace the evil skunks right now?"

Longarm let out a mildly derisive chuckle. "Stroll over, you bet. Brace 'em? Not sure about that. Wouldn't want to face either man down in a lead-pitchin' contest unless I just absolutely had no other choice. Possibility of havin' to draw on both of 'em at the same time should give the most accomplished pistolero in Tejas pause."

"Sure enough sends icy shivers up and down my spine."

"Well, don't let it bother you too much, Hamp. I have no such lunacy in mind today. We'll just stroll on down that way for a bit of semifriendly palaverin'. Shouldn't be a problem. Truth is, I can't wait to hear the tale they're gonna tell 'bout what they were doing last night. Yessir, that one oughta be a windy whizzer of the first water."

Custis Long flashed Forbes a toothy, friendly grin, then slapped his jughead's rump. He resettled the three-and-a-half-pound chunk of death-dealing iron at his waist, then set to legging it for Jennings Bugg and Fast Eddie's roost near the Big River Saloon's front entrance. Midway of the street, it suddenly occurred to him that Val Verde's usually bustling main thoroughfare was nigh on deserted. The distinct dearth of walkers, riders, wagons, and shoppers sent a prickling sensation of gooseflesh and sudden dread crawling up the back of his neck.

Dozen or so steps from their objective, Longarm cast a quick, pointed glance at Bugg and Bloodsworth from beneath the brim of his snugged-down, snuff-colored Stetson. Appeared as though Fast Eddie had realized that heavily armed lawmen were headed his direction. The surly thug hopped to his feet and backed into a spot beside and about half a step behind Jennings Bugg's shade-covered seat. It was the same protective maneuver Longarm had seen Bloodsworth make when the Tyler clan had confronted the insolent pair of killers inside the saloon the previous afternoon.

Over his shoulder, Longarm said, "Looks to me like the word about Drew Tyler's midnight lynchin' might have already got around town, Hamp."

"Wouldn't surprise me," Forbes said. "Have to admit, it'd be right odd if somebody else hadn't passed by before we got to him. For all I know, a dozen people could've already seen the corpse. Someone's likely made the same connection to Bugg and Bloodsworth we did. Probably told everyone in sight, and then the whole bunch of them headed out of the range of prospective gunfire."

Longarm stopped at the edge of the Big River's piece of boardwalk. Stood within spitting distance of Jennings Bugg's single-plank throne—a thick, stool-like affair made of oak rubbed shiny by the sweating behinds of untold numbers of Val Verde ranchers, cowboys, and run-of-the-mill loafers.

Longarm hoisted a booted foot onto the raised, rough-cut, dust-covered walkway and casually crossed one arm over his knee.

Hamp Forbes, shotgun nestled in the crook of his arm, silently drew up near his fellow lawman's left elbow. A bloodred curtain of palpable tension dropped between the marshals and the men loafing on the Big River's covered veranda.

Chapter 17

The burning itch of imminent calamity returned to the sweaty nape of Longarm's neck. In the most affable tone he could muster, the apprehensive lawman said, "Well, well, well. Looks like you boys were busier'n a couple of one-eyed dogs in a meat market last night. Huh, Jennings?"

For several dragging seconds, Jennings Bugg didn't bother to look up. He picked at a dirt-encrusted fingernail with a pocketknife. Let out something that sounded like a cross between a grunt and a mocking chuckle. "Always somethin' with you lawdogs, ain't it? Cain't seem to have a day's peace without some a you sons a bitches wanna cause me grief. Hotter'n hell on Sunday out here. Ain't even hardly a breeze blowin' to help cool a feller down a bit. Then you two idjets turn up talkin' some kinda unintelligible trash. Just what'n the hell 'er you goin' on about, Long?"

"You know full well what I'm talkin' about. Figure both of you know."

Bugg pushed against the unpainted board-and-batten wall at his back and brought his chin up. Slow, like a venomous snake waking in the cold. Thin, contemptuous lips curled away from yellowed tobacco-stained teeth as he glared down into the street at the lawmen. "No. Can't say as I do." Then, without taking his dead-eyed gaze off Longarm, he added, "You have any idea what this here federal marshal's talkin' about, Eddie? Appears to me as though he's tryin' to insinuate somethin' 'bout us bein' *busy* last night. Whatever'n the hell that means."

Bloodsworth rolled a smoldering, well-chewed cheroot stub from one corner of his mouth to the other. He arched a deeply split, scab-covered eyebrow. "Ain't got the slightest fuckin' idea, Jennings. I slept the whole night through like a newborn babe. Didn't even have to get up and use the chamber pot, as a matter of pure fact. Have no memory of stirrin' outta my bed for a single second."

Longarm let a toothy grin etch its way across his face. Tried to sound sociable when he said, "Truth is, we can't prove anything. Not yet anyway. So you can deny all you like. But surely the pair of you have to be aware that you've crossed way and the hell over the line with this latest killin'."

Tense as a stalking wolf, forearms resting on the butts of his Hickok-styled pistols, Bloodsworth eased a few inches closer to Jennings Bugg, then growled, "Exactly what killing would that be, Marshal?"

"Why, the midnight lynchin' of Drew Tyler, of course. Poor dead bastard's danglin' from the thickest limb of Val Verde's hanging tree as we speak. Corpse's all bloated up. Tongue swole outta the side of his mouth. Damned thing looks like it's the size of a saddle blanket. Pants fulla dried, stinkin' offal. Big ole blackbirds peckin' at his unseeing eyes. Hellish sight, boys. Just hellish."

A faintly detectable, self-satisfied grin flitted around the corners of Jennings Bugg's razor-thin lips, then quickly vanished. "Why, I'm shocked," he said. "Shocked and amazed, I do declare. Drew Tyler lynched. Damned shame, you ask me, Marshal Long. He seemed like such a friendly, pleasant, vital young feller when we last saw him. Dead, you say? Strung up to the hanging tree? Cryin' damned shame. Yessir, sure as hell is."

Longarm gifted the nervy outlaw with a big, friendly grin, but deep down inside, his burning fuse had shortened considerably. "Where's your sister, Jennings?"

The corner of Bugg's eye twitched. "Uh, well, figure she's in her room at the hotel. Don't think the girl got much sleep last night. Mighta had a rough go of it. 'Course I wouldn't know for sure 'less I spoke with her first."

Longarm's make-believe grin broadened. "Soon as the remaining Tylers find out about Drew, they're gonna hit town with blood in their eyes this go-round, boys. Ain't gonna be no puttin' 'em off. 'Specially since they're already persuaded as how you fellers are responsible for their brother Wade's passing as well. Sincerely doubt that me'n Hamp'll be able to stop 'em again. 'Specially since the riders for their brand outnumber us about twenty to one."

Bugg stabbed his knife into the shiny plank seat of the wooden bench, glared down at Longarm, and hissed, "Had my drothers, Long, I'd a-said you shouldn'a stopped 'em last time around when they showed up lookin' for trouble. This damned dance could've already been over and done with by now. The whole buncha them Tylers, the people responsible for my brother Charlie's death, I might remind you, could be pushin' up daisies out on boot hill as we speak. Me'n Bathsheba and Eddie could've been on our merry way to the mountains of New Mexico, Colorado, Wyoming, or wherever. But no-o-o: You law-bringin' bastards just had to step in and keep nature from takin' its preordained course. This steamin'-fresh cow pie of a mess woulda been sorted out and done with if you boys had just stayed the hell out of our way."

Jennings Bugg's mouthy arrogance flew all over Longarm. He had heard enough. Growing angrier by the second, he pulled away from the boardwalk and straightened up. Shot an angry, pointed glare in Bugg's direction that could have blistered paint off a New Hampshire barn door. From behind a death-dealing squint, he snarled, "Now listen to me, you son of a bitch. Me'n Marshal Forbes are takin' all bets that the remaining Tylers, along with a sizable contingent of Twisted T riders, are gonna come stormin' into town sometime before noon today and blast the hell out of you two murderous fuckers. Town's had enough killin' over the past few weeks to last a decade or more. Know you're not especially open to advice, but why don't you two jackasses saddle up and ride the hell on outta here before anyone else meets with some kind of strange, bizarre, or unfortunate end. Be sure and take your sister with you."

With the nervous spasm violently jerking at the corner of one eye, Jennings Bugg came to his feet like a mountain lion just before attacking its prey. In a half-crouch, hands hovering above his weapon's oiled walnut grips, he squinted hard at Longarm. "You want some of me and my friend here, Long? Wanna go for that big pistol layin' 'crost your belly, lawdog? Hell, you can put an end to this dance right here, right now. All you gotta do is kill me and Fast Eddie. Come on and get some, lawdog. Do it. Pull that smoke pole and get to work. Otherwise, get the hell outta my face."

Longarm flicked an earth-scorching gaze back and forth between Bugg and his lethal companion. Death had sidled up into their midst and was leaning against his black-handled, blood-soaked scythe, waiting and watching. Watching to see how many of the four men hunched over their guns out front of Val Verde's Big River Saloon he would drag down to a sulfurous hell with him.

Damn, might have pushed the crazy bastard too far, Longarm thought. Off to his left, he heard Hamp Forbes thumb the hammers back on the .10-gauge Greener. The distinctly separate pair of metallic snaps were so loud, they sounded like someone breaking cottonwood limbs with a double-bit ax.

Surprised Longarm when he felt, rather than saw, Forbes swing the shotgun around and level the weapon's massive muzzle up on the pair of bowed-up gunmen on the porch. Gore-saturated image of the four of them lying in the street, all shot to pieces, exploded across the backs of Custis Long's eyes.

As calmly as he could manage, Longarm brought his hands up in the classic gesture of appeasement. He made a near-undetectable motion toward Hamp Forbes, then said, "Easy now, boys. You, too, Hamp. No need for gunplay. Not just now anyway. We just stopped by to let you know what you could expect as a result of what Marshal Forbes and I just found out on the edge of town. So, let's all just calm down."

Calm as the darkest shadow at the bottom of a posthole, Forbes said, "Let the troublemaking skunks go on ahead and draw, Long. First finger touches a pistol butt, I'm gonna drop both these hammers. Double-barreled load of buckshot will splatter both of them all over the Big River's front facade. From this distance, won't be enough left of either one of these stupid sons of bitches to sweep up on a barkeep's dustpan."

Jennings Bugg recoiled as though someone had slapped him across the mouth. He blinked, then darted a nervous tongue tip across dry, cracked lips. Fast Eddie Bloodsworth took a barely perceptible half step backward. Quicker than double-geared lightning, the demeanor of both men shifted for the better.

Bugg's nervous gaze shooting back and forth between Longarm and Forbes, he came out of his crouch with great care. A tense smile sliced across the bottom half of his near chinless jaw. Both hands snapped to the buckle on his pistol belt, in an obvious signal of submission.

"Careful, now, Marshal Forbes," Bloodsworth said. "Wouldn't want you to touch that big popper off by accident. Might end up killin' both us ole boys deader'n Santa Anna."

Longarm took a single, deliberate step backward. Without looking, he extended one arm and carefully placed a rock-steady hand atop the barrels of Hamp Forbes's man killer. As Forbes lowered the weapon, Longarm said, "Gonna let your belligerent behavior pass this time 'round, Bugg. But trust me on this one, there ain't gonna be a next time. You ever threaten me again, and I'll gun the both of you so fast you'll be in hell shovelin' hot coals before you can blink twice."

With one arm extended across Hamp Forbes's chest, Longarm backed his way down the street and forced Val Verde's angry, teeth-gritting lawman along with him. Once past the entrance of Bob's Big Canyon Café, both men turned and hoofed it to the welcoming patch of shade offered by the jail's covered front porch.

The edgy lawmen each selected a porch pillar, leaned against it, smoked, and kept a wary lookout down the street on Bugg and Bloodsworth. An hour passed. Then two. Tired of standing, Longarm dragged a chair from the marshal's outer office onto the porch.

He'd just flopped into his seat, stoked a nickel cheroot to life, and propped a foot against one of the veranda's four-by-four roof supports, when he sighted Doc Hughes guiding his fancy cabriolet to a stop outside Val Verde's infirmary. Nettie sat in the seat beside her father. Even from a distance of nearly ninety feet, Longarm could easily detect the girl's tired, haggard appearance. Dark circles beneath her turquoise eyes bespoke a grueling few days out in the rough West Texas countryside. Woman looked as tired as a cat that had just tried to walk five miles in foot-deep mud.

When Longarm stood, the country doctor's handsome daughter immediately spotted his tall, distinct, muscular figure. And in spite of her obvious fatigue, she hopped from her father's carriage and hurried to his side.

"Where've you been, darlin'?" he said as she ran her arms around his waist and leaned a disheveled head against his chest. For some seconds, Longarm got no answer to his question.

Then, following a sigh that rose up from deep inside her breast, she finally said, "Family named Barlow has a ranch about thirty miles southwest of here, down near the Big Canyon River. Day before yesterday, a horse kicked their only son in the head. Fine young man named David. They felt it best not to move the poor boy any more than necessary. Sent word by a rider who arrived very early in the morning. And so, Father and I had to go out to the ranch."

"Kid okay?"

"No. He died. Passed away within hours of our arrival. We stayed over to help the family prepare the body and attend the funeral."

"Damn. That's a shame. Always hate to hear such news. 'Specially when it comes to the young'uns."

"Yes. He was exceptional. Well liked by everyone who knew him. I'm sure there are many who will mourn his passing once the news gets around."

"Well, I'm—" Longarm never finished his thought. The rumbling, rolling roar of clattering horses' hooves at the west end of Val Verde's stone-paved central thoroughfare drowned out whatever he'd intended to say, along with almost everything else important a body might have needed to hear.

Their faces covered with brightly colored bandannas, more than a dozen whooping, pistol-firing riders stormed into town. Windows shattered all along either side of the street as they passed. The near-empty street vibrated and echoed like an empty rain barrel being beaten with an ax handle.

Longarm grabbed Nettie's hand and turned for the jailhouse door. He'd taken but a single step toward safety when four or five members of the band of riders drew their mounts up, and spun them in tight circles in the street outside Hamp Forbes's office. They loosed a volley of gunfire that riddled the jail's walls. Boards in the building's painted wooden facade shattered and flew into a misty spray of thousands of flying splinters. The stout lockup's beveled, leaded glass window, with the words MARSHAL'S OFFICE painted on it in bloodred script, exploded in a cloud bank of sparkling, jagged fragments that resembled a fast-moving storm of diamonds thrown into the air.

Of a sudden, Nettie Hughes's hand became heavier than a boat anchor. Longarm dropped to one knee, then fell to his stomach and flattened out on the dusty boardwalk. He tried to pull the girl to his side, but she'd turned into deadweight. With wave after wave of smoking lead still crashing all around him, he knifed a glance backward. A sizable portion of the once beautiful Nettie's head had gone missing—replaced by a ragged mess of gore-matted hair, splintered bone, and exposed, blood-drenched brain matter.

"Goddammit," Longarm screeched. And despite a still-withering swath of blistering gunfire, he leaped to wobbling feet, snatched the girl into his muscular arms in a single motion, and stumbled through the jail's open doorway. Blue whistlers groaned, whizzed, and whined past on all sides, and a roiling fog of spent gunpowder enveloped the pair as he staggered to a spot on the far side of Hamp Forbes's desk and fell to his knees.

With hot lead chewing holes in every flat surface available, like a stirred nest of angry hornets, Longarm tenderly laid the broken Nettie out on the floor, then knelt beside her. Bits of paper, broken glass from the marshal's favorite coffee cup, wood splingers, a bullet-blasted ink blotter, and fragments from several desktop file trays rained down on the couple.

The swirling haze of acrid gun smoke pouring into the room grew more dense. Shots plinked off the iron bars of the jail's gated entrance. Then, as if by magic, Hamp Forbes came scurrying from behind his office safe and placed trembling fingers against the shattered Nettie's neck. Over the deafening din of gunfire, yelping shooters, clattering horses' hooves, exploding wallboards, furniture, and office fittings, he leaned into Longarm's ear and yelled, "Holy shit, Long. She's dead. Sweet Jesus. She's gone."

Longarm hit his feet so fast, Hamp Forbes was left on his knees to stare at Nettie's crumpled body, shake his head from side to side, pull his hair with both hands, and mumble like a madman. Longarm attacked the immobilized marshal's gun rack like a thing gone wild. He wrenched a pair of short-barreled shotguns from their slots. Holding one in each hand, he breeched them at the same time. Found both loaded with heavy-gauge buckshot.

The firestorm of indiscriminate blasting from the street slackened somewhat as Longarm snapped both the big poppers closed, then laid one weapon across his arm. He rummaged back and forth in the cabinet's only shelf, grabbed a half-empty box of shells, and dumped as many of them into his coat pocket as he could manage.

The discarded, empty shell box ricocheted off the still-kneeling Hamp Forbes's shoulder and instantly brought him out of his state of stunned stupefaction. He sprang to his feet and grabbed the only other Greener left propped in the doorless gun cabinet. He cast a final red-eyed glance at the limp body of Nettie Hughes, then followed Longarm through his hoosegow's bullet-riddled doorway and onto the boardwalk.

Longarm leapt from the wooden walkway into the alley between the jail and Bob's Café, then snugged up against the popular eatery's west-facing wall. He snuck a glance around the corner past Oldham's Wagon Yard, the Davis Brothers' Shoe Shoppe, and the Big Canyon Bank. All the action had moved to the street outside the Big River Saloon.

Amidst a cyclonic swirl of dust and churning waves of choking black-powder gun smoke, at least eight riders raged back and forth. Fired their weapons into the liquor locker's splintered batwings and obliterated front window. A number of motionless bodies decorated the dusty roadway. Here and there, horses, missing their riders, stood as though confounded by the furor, the tumultuous level of confusion and noise, the feverish activity, and the lack of someone on their backs.

A pair of animals lay unmoving in the middle of the street near the motionless bodies of their wounded, or perhaps dead, owners. Those men still horsed kicked their animals back and forth, or twirled in tight circles in an effort to dodge a withering sheet of return fire coming from low in the Big River's doorway and one corner of the saloon's now-missing front window.

Longarm cocked his head ever so slightly in Hamp Forbes's direction, but never once took his gaze off the violent, churning action in the street. "Gonna put an end to this once and for all. Soon's I step out into the street, Hamp, you can fall in with me or stay here. Whichever you choose, stay behind me where it's safe. If I have to fire, I intend on killin' everything in front of my guns."

Half a step into the street, Longarm hesitated. Forbes crashed into his back. Using one of the shotguns as a pointer, Longarm raised the weapon and said, "Look yonder. Appears as though the Tylers fell right into Jennings Bugg's well-laid trap. Someone's firing from a second-floor window 'cross the street over there in the Bishop Hotel. Be willin' to bet its Bathsheba. Most likely had us under the gun when we argued with Jennings and Bloodsworth earlier. Best be wary of getting shot in the back if she gets behind us now."

As Forbes followed Longarm into the street, he yelled, "You take care of whatever's in front of us, Long. I'll watch our backs."

The swarming throng of masked riders proved so preoccupied with the lethal cross fire they found themselves in that none of them noticed the pair of lawmen until it was way past too late. As though molded from a single bar of heat-tempered iron, Longarm strolled to a halt in the middle of the street between the Canyon Bank and the Bishop Hotel. With deadly deliberateness, he raised one of the shotguns and fired both barrels of fingernail-sized pellets directly into the teeming mass of inattentive riders. In an instant, he had tossed the spent weapon aside, and brought the second blaster up for deadly use.

Four of the masked men and two more horses went down as though struck by invisible bolts of lightning tossed from heaven by a vengeful God. The animals let out piteous squeals, lay on their sides, flopped, kicked, then ran in place. Their former riders appeared as if carved from stone, lying like lumps unable to move.

As though to himself, Longarm muttered, "Damnation, ain't nothin' I hate worse than havin' to shoot a good horse. But this shit has got to stop."

All but two of those riders unscathed by the lethal blast cast shocked glances the lawmen's direction. To a man, they twirled their hammerheads, then kicked for the safety of the tall and uncut, located somewhere out past the easternmost edge of town. Longarm quickly calculated that those fleeing the scene probably wouldn't stop heeling it until they got to Del Rio.

Pistols in hand, both the shrouded gunmen who had stayed behind, and obviously hadn't been hit by the death-dealing spray from Longarm's scattergun, leapt from their mounts' backs and ripped the bandannas away. Jack Tyler slanted a quick, wild-eyed glance toward his sister, Billie.

The crazed-looking girl nodded, then raised her chin and flicked the barrel of one of her weapons toward the saloon's entrance. Just then, Jennings Bugg and Fast Eddie Bloodsworth stepped through the devastated batwings, ambled across the boardwalk as though on a leisurely stroll to Sunday school, and moved into Val Verde's smoky main thoroughfare. A street that very much resembled a combination open-air slaughterhouse and graveyard.

From his vantage point nearly twenty feet away, Longarm cocked the still-charged Greener held in sweaty hands and watched as the quartet of belligerents squared off no more than ten feet away from each other. Billie Tyler yelled out, "You lawdogs stay the hell outta this. These men murdered our brothers. We intend to take no more than the justice they deserve to have visited on them for those killin's."

"Can't have it," Longarm yelled back, and took several aggressive steps closer to the action. "You, or some of the crazy sons a bitches ridin' with you, have managed to kill Nettie Hughes on your way to this showdown. All four of you'd best drop your weapons and turn yourselves over to Marshal Forbes for arrest forthwith. Otherwise, I'll kill the hell outta every fuckin' one of you."

Without looking Longarm's direction, Jennings Bugg yelled, "Well, you can fold that five ways and stick it up your ignert ass, Mr. Denver Lawdog. Me'n Fast Eddie have what's left of this murderin' bunch right where we want 'em. Ain't gonna be no arrestin' nobody today. First time one a these Tylers twitches. we're gonna—"

The .38-caliber slug delivered from the business end of Billie Tyler's silver-washed, ivory-gripped Colt Lightning pistol plowed into Jennings Bugg's head just above the bridge of his nose. The gunny's noggin snapped back, his hat flew off. Then, as though all the bones had been yanked out of his body in a single instant, he went to ground like a burlap bag of wet river sand.

Before anyone still left standing could've spit, Fast Eddie Bloodsworth screeched, "Goddamn all you Tylers straight to a festerin' hell." Then he thumbed off a torrent of murderous gunfire. Four, perhaps five, red-hot slugs slashed their way across Jack Tyler's chest like an Iowa farmer's hay sickle. Deadly accurate placement of shots put Tyler on his back as if someone had hit him in the breastbone with a railroader worker's spike-driving hammer.

Bloodsworth was in the midst of shifting his field of fire toward Billie Tyler when Hamp Forbes dropped both hammers of his Greener at the same instant. Near-deafening blast knocked the flabbergasted gunman out of both boots. Fast Eddie's limp, bug-eyed, twitching corpse landed on the Big River saloon's stretch of bullet-riddled boardwalk like it had been dropped from Heaven's front gate.

Bloodsworth's carcass still spasmed when Longarm caught sight of movement from the corner of one eye. Firing a Winchester model '73 rifle from the hip, Bathsheba Bugg advanced toward Billie Tyler. And while the last of the Bugg clan could for damn sure move shells through a lever-action rifle, her aim suffered from undue haste.

Billie Tyler appeared completely unconcerned by the ferocity of the attack. Bullets whizzed past the woman on every side as she brought her pair of Lightning pistols up, took careful aim, and delivered a stunning volley of pistol fire that set Bathsehba Bugg back on her heels, then knocked her onto her back.

The women couldn't have been more than fifteen feet away from each other when, lying on her back in the street only seconds away from death, Bathsheba Bugg squeezed off one final, devastating round that caught Billie Tyler in the throat just above the notch of her breastbone. Both twinkling pistols dropped from the stunned Billie's hands. She gagged on gouts of blood that instantly gushed from the chasm in her neck, went to her knees, pawed at the gaping wound, gazed at the sky for a few seconds like she might have been beseeching God, then collapsed in an unmoving heap.

Of a sudden, the world went so quiet, Longarm felt sure he could hear the tiny hairs growing in his ears.

Hamp Forbes dropped his arms to his side as though he might collapse, groaned, then said, "Sweet Merciful Jesus, have pity on us all."

Chapter 18

Marshal Billy Vail ran an already damp palm from the front of his sweaty, near-hairless pate to the back. He cast a tired gaze at Custis Long, tossed his deputy's lengthy handwritten report onto his desk, then let out an exasperated sigh. "Only managed to recover twenty thousand dollars of the government's stolen money?"

Slumped in Vail's lumpy, tack-decorated Moroccan leather guest chair, a haggard-looking Custis Long rubbed at the bluish black ring under one eye, then reached for the Stetson hanging on the toe of his boot and thumbed a speck of dirt off the brim. He absentmindedly scratched at the half inch of stiff stubble growing along one jaw. In agreement with his boss's pointed assessment, Longarm bobbled his head up and down as if he barely had enough reserve energy left to move.

"Accounting leaves a considerable amount of money still missing," said Billy. "You reckon there's any chance at all that we'll ever see any of the balance?"

Longarm shifted further down into the overstuffed chair's deep, comfortable cushions. Sounded as though he spoke from the bottom of an empty metal barrel when he said, "Doubt it, Billy. Charlie Bugg most assuredly hid the balance. Don't have a single clue where. Tried, but had no luck gettin' him to give up the location. From all available evidence, he didn't tell anyone else either. Not even them as were most likely with him during the robbery—his brother, sister, and Fast Eddie Bloodsworth."

"And you feel Jennings Bugg showed up in Val Verde looking for his brother so he could get all that loot back?"

"Of course. But then Jennings and Bathsehba found out how Charlie died and, God Almighty, that ripped the rag off the bush for sure. Whole murderous dance out in Val Verde's main thoroughfare came about as an indirect result of that pile of ill-gotten loot's disappearance."

Vail closed both eyes and shook his head.

"Damned cash could be buried anywhere, Billy. Beneath any rock, bush, or stump spread out over a thousand-mile stretch between the scene of the robbery and ole Charlie's hotel room in Buckhorn, Texas. Money's gone, Boss. Probably gone forever. Only way anyone'll ever see a dime of that plunder again is by sheer, blind-lucky chance."

Vail snatched his still-smoking Cuban cigar from the cut-glass ashtray atop his overburdened desk, took a puff, then said, "And how many people ended up dead?"

Longarm rolled his eyes toward the ceiling as though hopeful the Diety might be hiding in one of the room's corners and could float down and give him some guidance. "Well, let's see," he said, then moved to the edge of his seat and groaned as though suffering from a gut-twisting case of unsettled bowels. "If we start with the original murder of Buster Tyler, then count the unfortunate lynchin' of Charlie Bugg. Add in Wade Tyler, poor bastard Hamp Forbes and I both think was most likely beaten to death, then shot several times just for good measure. And then go and tack on Drew Tyler, who we know for certain was lynched à la Charlie Bugg. Throw the ill-fated death of Nettie Hughes into the mix, along with Jack Tyler, Jennings Bugg, Fast Eddie Bloodsworth, Billie Tyler, Bathsheba Bugg, and half a dozen or so miscellaneous Twisted T riders, think that comes to something like, oh, lemme see. You add your one and your two, then you carry the—"

Billy Vail sounded like he wanted to spit up a hairball the size of a number-ten galvanized washtub when he grunted, "Sixteen people, Custis. Telegram I got from Marshal Forbes confirmed fifteen, and if you tack on Buster Tyler, that's sixteen."

"Sounds close enough to raise a blister to me. Not countin' all the horses, of course."

"No arrests."

"No one left alive to throw in jail. All them as we could determine might have some responsibility for one killin' or another were dead, dead, dead."

Vail leaned back in his chair and clenched his eyes shut for a second, then said, "Christ Almighty, Custis, fifteen people rubbed out in less than a week. Most of them on a single blood-soaked afternoon."

"Shit, Billy, no call lookin' at me like that. Shots I fired didn't manage to put lead in but four of them as was raisin' all the hell. I only touched off two barrels of buckshot in an effort to try and stop the massacre before it got any worse than it already was. Two of those ole boys I brought down survived. 'Course both of 'em got peppered pretty good. Doc took enough pellets out of one of 'em to make a set of sinkers for a fishin' net, but both of 'em lived, by God."

"Lot of folks down that way, especially hard-nosed newspaper editors, are already referring to that shocking afternoon of blood as 'the Val Verde massacre.'"

Longarm pulled a nickel cheroot from his vest pocket and, without lighting the cigar, laid it into the corner of his mouth. He chewed on the stogie for a few seconds, pushed it back into place with his tongue, then said, "Val Verde mass-a-cree, huh? Well, Billy, if the blood-soaked event that occurred that day wasn't a mass-a-cree, it'll damn sure do till the real mass-a-cree comes along."

Vail rolled his eyes in dogged resignation, then with a

sudden degree of something approaching sympathy seeping into his voice, said, "Got the impression from portions of your report that you'd grown somewhat attached to that unfortunate Hughes woman. Hints were subtle, I'll grant, but I did find some in there."

Longarm picked at a patch of invisible lint on the leg of his pants, stared droopy-eyed at the banjo clock on the wall, then stood, tiredly stuffed his Stetson back on, and said, "Nettie and I had potential, Billy. We just never got the chance to realize whatever might have been ahead for us."

As Billy Vail's favorite deputy strode for the office door like a man dragging a dead elephant, the ruddy-faced U.S. marshal said, "Where you goin' now, Custis?"

Longarm stopped in his boss's open entryway and leaned against the door frame. Absentmindedly stared at the floor and said, "Think I'll perambulate on down to the Holy Moses Saloon. Place is like my second home these days. Have Mike O'Hara pour me double shots of Gold Label Maryland Rye till I'm so whiskey weary I can't raise a glass anymore."

"Should I have someone come by later who can help get you home?"

"Aw, hell, no, Billy. Figure if I should manage to pass out sittin' at the table, Cora Anne Fisher'll take mercy on my poor sad ass and see to it I get carried upstairs to pass the night in her bed. But if anything comes up and you need to send for me, that's where I'll be holed up."

Vail stared at Longarm's gaunt profile. "Suppose each man has his very own individual method of chasing the ghosts of the past away."

"Yeah," Longarm said, then heeled it for the Denver Federal Building's second-floor hallway and descending staircase. Over his shoulder, but more to himself than anyone else, he called out, "Sure as hell can't shoot 'em."

DON'T MISS A YEAR OF

Slocum Giant
by
Jake Logan

Slocum Giant 2004:
Slocum in the Secret Service

Slocum Giant 2005:
Slocum and the Larcenous Lady

Slocum Giant 2006:
Slocum and the Hanging Horse

Slocum Giant 2007:
Slocum and the Celestial Bones

Slocum Giant 2008:
Slocum and the Town Killers